"What am I going to d

It was hard to get the words p̲a̲s̲t̲ ̲h̲e̲r̲ ̲l̲i̲p̲s̲.

"What do you want to do, Olina?"

"I don't have the money to go back to Sweden."

Gustaf stood and walked over to the window. "I came to take you to Litchfield with me."

"Do your *moder* and *fader* want me to come?"

Gustaf turned from the window. He looked at her, but she didn't read pity in his expression. "Yes. They're not happy about what Lars did."

Olina sat up straighter. "What exactly did Lars do?"

"Didn't he write you at all after he went to Denver?"

"Denver?" Olina quickly stood and paced across the floor. "The last letter I received from him contained the money for my passage." She stopped walking and turned toward Gustaf. "What is he doing in Denver?"

"I don't want to talk about Lars right now." Gustaf stomped to the window again. "He's always making messes and leaving them for me to clean up. You are one of those messes, and I will take care of you, as I have all the others."

Olina could hardly believe her ears. "Did you just call me a mess?" She stood a little taller, the starch returning to her backbone. "I'm not sure I want to spend any time with you."

"Well, you're going to have to. . .until we get to Minnesota, at least!"

Why was he shouting at her? Did he want everyone in the hotel to know what had happened to her?

Olina walked over to the door. "I'll thank you to leave my room."

LENA NELSON DOOLEY is a free-lance author and editor who lives with her husband in Texas. During the years she has been a professional writer, she has been involved as a writer or editor on a variety of projects—a newspaper; a TV movie and public service announcements; curriculum for public school, private schools, children's Sunday school, and children's church for three different denominations; international business reports; and sketches for a Christian comedian. She developed a seminar called "Write Right," and she hosts a writing critique group in her home. She presently serves as a communication director, curriculum coordinator, and bookstore manager for her church. She has a dramatic ministry that crosses denominational lines and an international Christian clowning ministry. She and her husband enjoy taking vacations in Mexico, visiting, and working with missionary friends.

HEARTSONG PRESENTS

Books by Lena Nelson Dooley
HP54—Home to Her Heart

The Other Brother

Lena Nelson Dooley

Heartsong Presents

This book is dedicated to my two daughters, Marilyn Van Zant and Jennifer Waldron, who provided the catalyst that started me writing inspirational romance novels. Now they have given me the four most wonderful grandchildren in the world. And no book is ever written in our home without the support of my wonderful husband, James, whom I love more today than I ever imagined when I married him in 1964. He is the second most wonderful gift God ever gave me.

A note from the author:
I love to hear from my readers! You may correspond with me by writing:

> **Lena Nelson Dooley**
> **Author Relations**
> **PO Box 719**
> **Uhrichsville, OH 44683**

ISBN 1-58660-605-0

THE OTHER BROTHER

All Scripture quotations are taken from the King James Version of the Bible.

All of the characters and events in this book are fictitious. Any resemblance to actual persons, living or dead, or to actual events is purely coincidental.

Cover design by Dick Bobnick.

PRINTED IN THE U.S.A.

one

April 1891

Olina Sandstrom stood by the railing of the *North Star,* her face
turned away from the biting wind. A wayward curl persistently
crept from her upswept hairdo and fluttered against her chilled
cheeks. The wind flapped the hem of her heavy traveling suit
as well, threatening to sweep her into the choppy sea. Thank
goodness for the ship's railing. Even though the hard metal
chilled her fingers until they were almost numb, she didn't
want to let go.

The dark gray waters of the Atlantic Ocean spread from
horizon to horizon. The ocean seemed to be a living thing,
constantly moving and changing, never still. As waves lapped
against the dark hull of the ocean liner, the deck where she
stood dipped and rose in rhythm. It had taken Olina over a
day to get used to the feeling. The movement unsettled more
than her stomach. Never before had her foundation constantly
shifted.

Oh, to be on land again, to feel safe. But would she ever
feel safe again? Although Olina was excited to be on the
grand adventure that would culminate in her reunion with her
beloved, her heart was heavy with knowing what she had
given up. Knowing what she left behind, maybe forever.

The ocean fascinated Olina. Lars Nilsson's eyes were that
shade of gray, and they were always alive with plans and new
ideas. Even during storms, which had occurred more than
once in the week since they had left Sweden, the ocean

reminded Olina of Lars. When he was unhappy, his eyes took on that same brooding darkness. But when he was happy, they danced and flashed as the waves did when the sun sparkled across them. So day after day, Olina stood by the rail of the ship and longed for the time when she would look into those eyes again. It had been so long since she had seen them. This crossing seemed to be never ending.

"What are you looking at?" The soft voice of Johanna Nordstrom, Olina's traveling companion, penetrated Olina's concentration.

Olina gave a soft reply without looking away from the water that surrounded the ship. "The ocean."

"What do you find so interesting out there?" Johanna turned toward the churning water. Johanna had spent most of her time on the ship inside one of the salons. She told Olina that she preferred the warmth to the cold deck. Even in second class, the ship seemed luxurious to both of the young women.

Olina turned to face Johanna, one hand finally leaving the rail to swipe at a tendril that tickled her nose. "It reminds me of Lars. This voyage can't end soon enough for me. It has been so long since I saw him."

Looking out across the waves, Olina pictured Lars the last time they had been together. They had been alone in their favorite meadow. Soft green grass, dotted with tiny white flowers, spread around them. Jagged rocks broke through the ground cover farther up the slope, and the sound of the water in the *fjord* was a constant background melody punctuated by the calls of the birds that circled in the cerulean sky.

Lars came to tell her good-bye. When Olina started to cry, Lars pulled her into his arms. His gentle kiss brushed the hair from her temple. She didn't want to think of life without Lars. Ever since they were very young, they had known they would someday marry. Lars was an essential part of her. How could she go on without seeing him almost every day?

America was so far away. So far that she couldn't even imagine the distance. She just knew they would never see each other again. And it had taken years. Five long years.

"I'll work," Lars whispered against her coronet of braids, "and I'll save up until I can send you the money to come to America. Then we will be married. Even if it takes years, it'll be worth it." Lars placed a gentle kiss upon her willing lips before he left to meet his family at the docks.

Olina stayed in the meadow the rest of the afternoon. She relived every precious moment they had spent together. Every few minutes, she had touched the lips his tender kiss had covered for the first time, lost in the wonder of it.

"You know, Olina." Johanna's voice interrupted Olina's memories. "I haven't questioned you about your quick decision to accompany me to America. All you told me was that Lars had sent you the money for passage." Johanna patted one of Olina's icy hands. "I don't understand why none of your family came to see you off."

Olina wondered what she could tell her friend without making *Fader* sound bad. But Johanna deserved the truth. Without her help, Olina wouldn't be making this journey.

After turning away from the frothy water, Olina leaned on the railing, her hands still clutching it for support. "I wasn't trying to be mysterious. I just had a hard time talking about it." Thinking about it caused tears to pool in her eyes. She reached one hand into the pocket of her skirt and took out her pristine linen handkerchief to dab the tears away. "Fader didn't want me to go to America. He didn't understand. I love Lars so much, and there is no one else who can stir my heart as he does. I had to go to Lars."

Olina swallowed a sob. "Fader told me that I was old enough to make my own decision. . .but if I went, he would disown me. No one in my family would ever be allowed to contact me. *Tant* Olga said he didn't mean it, so I waited awhile before I made my decision, hoping he would change his mind. He didn't." Olina wept so hard that she could not continue her explanation.

"He probably didn't mean it. He thought you would do what he wanted." Johanna pulled Olina into her arms and let her cry. "He'll change his mind when you get to America, and you can tell him how happy you are. If not then, at least when you and Lars have children, he'll want to know his grandchildren."

Olina was warmed by the embrace. Her mother often hugged her when she was still living at home. She hadn't realized how much she had missed it.

When Olina stopped crying, she moved from Johanna's embrace and dried her face with her handkerchief. "*Tack så.* A good friend you are, for sure."

The ship dipped, and Johanna grabbed the railing. "I'm sorry I didn't realize something was wrong. I was excited about going to America to be with Olaf. Even though I'm married, my mother didn't want me to travel alone."

Olina tried to smile at her friend. "You and Olaf hadn't been married long when he went to America, *ja?*"

"Only a few months."

"It must have been hard for you."

Johanna nodded. "It was. But your decision was a difficult one, too. I'm not sure I could have made it."

Olina studied the waves with their whitecaps. "It was the hardest thing I've ever done, choosing Lars over my family."

৵

Gustaf Nilsson was angrier than he had been in a long time. "*Gud,* why did You let this happen?" When he was alone, Gustaf often talked to God. Was he ever alone today. Driving his wagon across the rolling plains in Minnesota toward Litchfield, all he could think about was taking the train to New York City.

Five years ago when his family had left New York, headed toward Minnesota, Gustaf had vowed never to set foot in that town again. It was too big for him. It was too dirty. . .and too noisy. . .and too crowded with people. Not at all the sort of place he wanted to be. He didn't like to be hemmed in. He needed fresh, clean air. He was a farmer. He tilled the land. And there was a Swedish settlement in Minnesota. That was why they had emigrated.

The winter before the move had been harder than usual in Sweden. With the crop failure that summer, the family finally heeded the pleas of their friends, who were already landowners in America, and sold everything they owned. God had been good to them in Minnesota. They bought a large farm, which Gustaf and Papa couldn't run alone. They had to hire several men to help them.

August, Gustaf's younger brother, had wanted to be a blacksmith. Papa thought it was a good idea, so August had moved to town. Then there was Lars, his youngest brother. Gustaf didn't want to think about Lars and what he had done. He didn't like to be this angry, but every time he thought of Lars, anger bubbled up inside him like the spring that had fed icy water to the family on their farm back in Sweden. But the anger did not cool him. It made him grow hotter and hotter. Even though the spring winds still blew, they couldn't touch the heat that was building in Gustaf.

"Fader, what am I going to do when I get there?" Gustaf looked into the wide blue sky, but the puffy white clouds didn't tell him anything. And he didn't hear the voice of God thundering the answer. Not that he expected it to. Gustaf had never heard the audible voice of God. He knew some people claimed to, but Gustaf always heard God's voice speak deep within his soul. That was where he hoped to hear something, but God was quiet today.

Why did Gustaf always have to clean up the messes Lars made? He knew he was the oldest, but that didn't mean he should have to leave the farm, where he had so many things that needed to get done, and travel to that awful place to meet that girl. Why hadn't she stayed in Sweden where she belonged? What would he do with the sturdy farm girl?

When the Nilssons had first arrived in Minnesota, the spring had been so wet that the roads were impassable. Lars had tried to go to town anyway. By the time Gustaf pulled the bogged-down wagon out of the mud, one of the axles had broken. He had taken it to town for August to fix before Papa found out. He hadn't minded that too much. Gustaf was glad August hadn't caused trouble like Lars had. One brother giving him grief was enough.

After a year, Lars decided he needed to work in town to make money to send for Olina. At first, Gustaf had been unhappy about that. So much of the time, Lars didn't complete what he was supposed to on the farm, and Gustaf was the one who finished the job. It was easier to do the whole thing himself. Besides, his sister, Gerda, helped more than Lars ever had.

Since he hardly ever finished anything he started, Gustaf had been sure that Lars would give up on the idea before he had earned enough money. That hadn't been the case. Lars took to merchandising. Before long, Mr. Braxton gave him more responsibility. Although it had taken another four years for Lars to save enough money to pay for Olina's passage, he never deviated from that plan. Then six months ago, Lars had sent Olina the money.

Soon after the letter was mailed, Mr. Braxton's brother from

Denver came to Litchfield. He had been impressed with Lars's abilities, so he offered him a position in his mercantile. Lars moved to Denver. He said he would be better able to provide for a family with the increased income. The whole Nilsson family assumed that Lars had written Olina about the change in plans.

It took a long time for mail to cross half of the United States, the ocean, and part of Europe. However, Gustaf had expected to hear before now that Olina had arrived in Denver. He didn't know why it took her so long to start the journey. Yesterday, they had received two messages. A letter from Lars and a telegram from Olina to Lars. Papa had opened the telegram because he thought it might be something important.

Olina's note told them when she would be arriving on the *North Star* in New York City. The letter from Lars was disturbing. He had fallen in love with Mr. Braxton's daughter, and they would be married by the time the letter reached Minnesota. He said he had only thought he loved Olina. Until he met Janice, he had not known what real love was. He would write to Olina and explain things, but Gustaf knew it was too late for that. Olina was already on her way when Lars wrote the letter, if he did.

Papa should have been the one to go to New York to meet Olina, but Mama didn't feel well. She had been extremely upset by the letter from Lars. Gustaf was sure that was the reason she felt so bad. She begged Papa to send Gustaf, so here he was.

Gustaf had half a mind to send Olina back where she came from. He would if she had enough money for the passage. He certainly didn't.

This would never have happened if Lars hadn't started working in that store. Why couldn't he love the farm as much as Gustaf did? Or if he had to work in a store, why had Lars not stayed in Litchfield with Mr. Braxton and his mercantile? Why did Lars wait to leave town until after he had sent Olina the money to come to Minnesota?

It was a good thing Gustaf's horses knew the way to town without much help from Gustaf. If they hadn't, he would have never made it to the train on time.

❧

The seemingly never-ending journey was finally over. The ship docked at something called the Battery in New York. Such a huge place it was. So many docks. So many ships. So many people. Olina was overwhelmed. She had never heard such a din in all her life. It was so loud it was hard to distinguish one sound from another—voices speaking in many languages, which Olina couldn't understand, clanging, banging, the hooting of ship's horns, the clatter of horses' hooves on the brick streets.

"It's a good thing we came when we did." Johanna looked out over the crowd that had gathered as the ship docked. It was a constantly moving sea of humanity.

"What do you mean?" Olina took time out from trying to find Lars in the crowd to look at her friend. "What difference would another time make?"

Johanna turned toward Olina. "I was talking to one of the other passengers. She told me that there are so many people coming to America that they are building a place on an island where they will process many of the emigrants. It's called Ellis Island, and it will be open for business in a few months. It'll take longer to be processed there before you get to come ashore. I want to be with Olaf as soon as possible." Just then she spied her husband's tall frame pushing through the crowd. She raised her hand as high as she could and waved her handkerchief.

❧

It had taken long enough to get off the ship and through

Immigration—much longer than either woman wanted it to take. But now Johanna was hanging onto Olaf's arm as Olina scanned the thinning crowd for Lars. Where could he be? She had sent a telegraph message before she boarded the ship. Surely he received it. It wasn't pleasant waiting here. Of course with fewer people around, Olina wasn't overcome with the strong smell of unwashed bodies as she had been when they first stepped on shore, but there were other unpleasant odors. Garbage and human waste were too strong for the ocean breezes to cleanse. Many of the men must have been drinking in nearby taverns before they came to the wharf. Stale alcohol mingled with all the other smells. Besides, the large ships blocked many of the breezes. There was also the odor of fish and fumes from the many boats. Olina thought about covering her nose with her handkerchief as some of the other women on the dock were doing, but she didn't.

❧

Gustaf had lost his good humor before he left home. Now it was so far away he didn't know if he would ever find it again. He was angry and frustrated. The train ride had been long and noisy. No one could sleep with all the babble from the passengers. Add to that the chugging engine and the *clackity-clack* of the rails. Gustaf had nursed a headache since he left Minnesota. The stuffy cars didn't help him feel any better. When he went out on the platform between cars to get a whiff of air, it wasn't fresh. Smoke from the engine, which enveloped the train itself, was no more pleasant than the unwashed bodies and bad breath inside the car. When he turned to go back inside, a cinder caught in the corner of his eye. After he removed it, tears formed in the injured eye for over an hour. For sure, he didn't want people to think he was crying.

When he had finally reached New York, it was a race against the other passengers to find a cabby who could take him to the docks. He had gotten the slowest cabby in New York City.

"Hey." Gustaf reached up and tapped the driver on the shoulder.

The driver didn't take his attention off the road. "Sir?"

"You aren't driving around and around trying to make my fare larger, are you?" Gustaf didn't try to disguise his anger.

"No, this is the most direct route to the Battery. That's where you said you was going, ain't it?" The man leaned away from a right turn, easily controlling the horses and buggy. "It's not far now."

"I'm glad." Gustaf scooted back in the seat, holding on tight. If not, he might be thrown from the buggy as it lurched and groaned its way through the traffic. "I'm meeting a young lady, and her ship should have docked over an hour ago."

"Why didn't you say so? We wouldn't want to leave a lady waiting in that mob." The man flicked the reins across the rumps of the horses, and they trotted at a much faster pace.

Gustaf glared blankly. He was trying to remember what Olina Sandstrom looked like. He didn't want to spend a lot of time looking for her. Blond braids loosely encircled her head the last time he saw her. She had a round face with rosy cheeks and big blue eyes. He thought Olina's eyes were the prettiest of any of the girls in their village. She helped her family with farm chores, so she was strong. Butter and cheese, from the family dairy, and rich pastries had kept her figure rounded. She should be easy to spot in New York. He hadn't seen that kind of girl anywhere he had been in the city.

"Here we are. Would you like me to wait to take you and your lady to a hotel?" The cabby looked around the area. "I don't see any other conveyance that ain't being used by some-one else."

"How much is that going to cost?" Gustaf could feel his

purse shrinking as they talked.

"Tell you what." The cabby winked down at him. "I wait for half an hour, and I won't charge nothing but the fare here and to where you're going. If you ain't back by then, I'll have to take any fare I can get."

"It's a deal."

Gustaf loped off, seething inside. The cheeky cabby thought he was coming for his own lady, not for his brother's castoff. If that didn't cap the day. Gustaf hurried toward the wharves, where he saw several ships docked. There was the vessel she had sailed on. Quickly, Gustaf scanned the scattered clusters of people near the *North Star*. Not one of the women looked like Olina. What if she hadn't boarded the ship? What if he had made the journey in vain? Gustaf's anger built even higher than it had been—if that were possible. Had he wasted all this time and money for nothing?

ᕒ

Once again, Olina looked around the large wharf area. Where was Lars? She didn't know what she would do if he didn't come. She had so little money left. Johanna had insisted that they book passage in second class. She didn't want to travel in steerage, where everyone was treated like cattle, sharing rooms and bathrooms and who knew what else. Olina had enjoyed the relative luxury. She knew it was not like first class, but she had never known that kind of life, so she didn't miss it. But she would have missed the money it would have cost. Olina didn't have that kind of money to start with. Now she almost wished she had talked Johanna into steerage. At least she would have enough money to make her way to Minnesota on her own if Lars was unable to meet her in New York.

"I wonder what's keeping Lars." Olaf turned from his conversation with Johanna to talk to Olina. "You could go with us to the hotel. I'm sure there's another room available. Of course, tomorrow we'll be leaving for Cincinnati, but we'd be glad to have you with us tonight."

Olina looked at Johanna, clutching her husband's arm as if she would never let go. She knew that the young couple didn't need her tagging along on their first night together in over a year.

"Lars wouldn't know where to find me if I went with you." Once again Olina looked around the wharf. "I think I'll wait a little longer."

"We can't leave you here alone." Johanna took Olina's arm. "It wouldn't be proper, and you might not be safe. I would worry instead of enjoying my husband." She smiled a secret smile at Olaf.

That smile made Olina uncomfortable, so she quickly looked away. That's when Olina noticed a man who seemed to be looking for someone. He was built like Lars, strong and muscular, and blond hair stuck out from under his navy blue cap. He looked a lot like Lars, but he was taller than she remembered Lars being. Maybe it was Lars. He could have grown taller since he had come to America. All that work and good food in the land of plenty. Maybe he had grown. Lars, or whoever he was, started toward them. Now he was close enough for her to see all of his face.

Just as Olina realized that, she looked into icy blue eyes. Sky blue and cold as the ice in the fjords in winter. They jolted her. But it wasn't Lars. His were gray, not blue.

❧

Gustaf recognized Olina's eyes the moment he saw them. It was a good thing. He would never have known who she was otherwise. She stood as if she were holding herself upright by the strength of her will. She was slender, with curves in all the right places. Instead of the braids he remembered encircling her head, her upswept hairdo was topped with a fashionable small hat that had ribbons and feathers and a small veil that was turned up. Wispy curls brushed her cheeks and neck.

Gustaf didn't know a lot about fashion, but he knew that the traveling suit she was wearing was fashionable. Olina had changed, all for the better. But she was fragile looking, as if the journey had worn her out. As if she would wilt if given the chance. He couldn't tell her what he had come to tell her until she had rested. He would have to wait for the right time. But what *was* the right time to tell a woman who had come halfway around the world that she had been jilted?

two

"Gustaf?" Olina was surprised she hadn't realized who he was right away.

He nodded as he glanced at the luggage. "How many of these are yours?"

"Those two trunks and this carpetbag." After Olina pointed out the pieces, she looked past Gustaf, scanning the thinning crowd. "Where—?"

"I have a cab waiting. We need to hurry." Gustaf hefted one trunk up on his back.

"Wait." Olina's hand on his arm stopped him. "I want you to meet my traveling companion and her husband." She turned toward the Nordstroms.

Olaf held out his hand. "I'm Olaf, and this is Johanna."

"I'm pleased to meet you." Gustaf let the trunk slip back to the dock before he shook Olaf's hand.

"Do we have to hurry to catch the train?" Olina had a lot of questions she wanted answered. "And is—?"

"No," Gustaf interrupted. "Our train doesn't leave until in the morning."

"But where will you spend the night?" Johanna sounded worried.

Olina smiled at her. How like Johanna to be more concerned for her friend than herself.

"I hadn't thought of that," Gustaf answered. "I guess I was planning on waiting at Grand Central Station tonight."

"Why don't you come to the hotel with us?" Olaf said. "I'm sure they have another room."

Gustaf looked angry, but he agreed. "We can share my cab if we hurry. The driver said he wouldn't wait long for us."

Each man picked up a trunk and started toward the cabstand, leaving the women to guard the other luggage. When they returned for the other two trunks, Olina and Johanna went with them, each carrying a carpetbag, as well as their reticules.

The cab was crowded. Olina had to sit very close to Gustaf. After they had gone a couple of blocks, she leaned close to his ear. "Where is—?"

"That's our hotel." Olaf pointed toward a three-story building with a red brick facade.

When the three men had unloaded the baggage, Olaf and Gustaf went to the front desk.

"I booked you a room on the same floor as your friends, but on the other side of the hotel," Gustaf told Olina when they returned. "My room is on the next floor."

As they walked across the lobby to the staircase, the carpet softened Olina's tired steps. It was a good thing Gustaf had brought her here. Olina wouldn't have been able to afford a hotel room at all in this big city. New York City. It was so confusing and noisy.

After the baggage was stored in the three hotel rooms, the four went to the restaurant on the ground floor. Another time, Olina would have enjoyed the beauty of the place, aglow with gas lights on the walls, as well as candles on each table. Delicious smells wafted through the room, making Olina aware that she had not eaten much that day. She had been too excited, knowing they were landing in New York. She was supposed to see Lars waiting for her. That had added to her excitement, but that had not happened. Now here she was in a hotel restaurant with Gustaf. Maybe he would soon tell her where Lars was and why he didn't come to meet her.

As soon as they were seated, a young woman in a long black dress with a white apron and cap served them. Gustaf and Olaf were able to converse with her in English. Neither Olina nor Johanna understood anything they said. But the two men sounded as if they had spoken the language all their lives. Olina hoped she would be able to learn the strange way of speaking. It felt uncomfortable being an outsider. Surely Lars could speak English as well as Gustaf. Lars would help her learn. He wouldn't want her feeling uncomfortable around others.

The meal was congenial, but Olina waited for Gustaf to bring up Lars's whereabouts. Lars hadn't even been mentioned during the meal. Gustaf seemed rather aloof. Maybe he didn't want to talk about Lars in front of the Nordstroms. Olina was beginning to worry. She hoped Lars was not sick or injured. Just wait until Gustaf walked her to her room. She would get to the bottom of this.

≈

All through the meal, Gustaf was distracted. He tried to carry on a sensible conversation with his companions, but his thoughts were otherwise engaged.

Here they were in a hotel, using up more of the hard-earned money he had brought with him. He felt each dollar as it slipped through his fingers, his precious store dwindling at an alarming rate. He had better get Olina back to the farm quickly, before he ran out of money. Why had he not brought more with him? He had enough put away that it wouldn't have hurt to bring extra so he wouldn't feel the pinch, but he had been angry. He only wanted to get the trip over with. He hadn't wanted to spend one penny more than was necessary, and he had planned to send Olina back to her parents. Besides, he would need his money when he and Anna married.

Gustaf hadn't thought about spending time at a hotel. He was going to go back to the train station and wait for the train to Minnesota, even if it took all night. When he first saw Olina standing there, he knew he couldn't treat her that way. Now look at the mess he was in. It was a good thing Fader had told him to buy both tickets before he left home. He had planned to turn Olina's ticket in and get his money back after he put her on a ship to Sweden. Now he barely had enough money for food until they got to Litchfield.

Gustaf hadn't even mentioned Lars to Olina. How could he bring up his name without exploding with anger? She didn't need to see that, not in her condition. She was so tired; she looked as if she was having a hard time staying awake. There was not one detail of her actions or appearance that escaped him.

If he could get his hands on Lars right now, he would likely hurt him. How could Lars do this to Olina? Why couldn't he be man enough to face this on his own?

Olina said she was hungry, but she didn't eat like the farm girl of his memory. She ate more like his mother did, with grace and poise. She had stopped eating before her plate was empty. She insisted the food tasted good, but she left some, as his mother often did.

What was he doing comparing her to his mother? Was he mad? How was he going to tell her about Lars? He would have to wait until the right time.

☙

When Gustaf finished the last bite on his plate, Olina stood up. "I'm tired." She looked right at him. "Will you walk me to my room?"

Olaf stood when Olina and Gustaf did. Then he sat back down with his wife.

At the top of the stairs, Olina could wait no longer. "Where is Lars?" she asked as they walked down the hall.

"I'm not sure."

Olina stopped and placed her hands on her hips. "What do you mean, you're not sure? Is something the matter with him?"

Anger blazed from Gustaf. "Yes, something's the matter with him. He's married."

Olina couldn't believe her ears. Surely he hadn't said what she thought she heard. "Married?"

She didn't realize she had voiced the question until she saw the expression on Gustaf's face. He reached toward her, but she stepped back from him.

"Olina, I'm sorry. I didn't mean to tell you this way." He took her arm, but she pulled away.

"How could he be married?" The question ended on a squeak. Here she was worried that Lars was sick or hurt, and he had done this to her. Olina clutched her arms around her waist as if something inside hurt. And it did. Everything hurt. She felt as if she couldn't stand up another minute.

Gustaf must have realized this, because he put his arms around her and pulled her against his chest. Olina began to sob. What was she going to do now?

Gustaf helped her walk to her room. "We need to talk. If we leave the door open, I can come in for a few minutes."

He eased her into a chair and hunkered on the floor beside her. Olina didn't look at his face. How could she? She didn't want to see pity there. First Fader rejected her, and now Lars had jilted her. How could God have let this happen?

"What am I going to do?" It was hard to get the words past the lump in her throat.

"What do you want to do, Olina?"

"I don't have the money to go back to Sweden."

Gustaf stood and walked over to the window. "I came to take you to Litchfield with me."

"Do your *moder* and *fader* want me to come?"

Gustaf turned from the window. He looked at her, but she didn't read pity in his expression. "Yes. They're not happy about what Lars did."

Olina sat up straighter. "What exactly did Lars do?"

"Didn't he write you at all after he went to Denver?"

"Denver?" Olina quickly stood and paced across the floor. "The last letter I received from him contained the money for my passage." She stopped walking and turned toward Gustaf. "What is he doing in Denver?"

"I don't want to talk about Lars right now." Gustaf stomped to the window again. "He's always making messes and leaving them for me to clean up. You are one of those messes, and I will take care of you, as I have all the others."

Olina could hardly believe her ears. "Did you just call me a mess?" She stood a little taller, the starch returning to her backbone. "I'm not sure I want to spend any time with you."

"Well, you're going to have to. . .until we get to Minnesota, at least!"

Why was he shouting at her? Did he want everyone in the hotel to know what had happened to her?

Olina walked over to the door. "I'll thank you to leave my room."

"All right. I'll go, but I'll be here to pick you up early in the morning so we can catch our train." At least he had moderated his tone. "When we get to Litchfield, you and my parents can decide what to do."

After Olina closed the door behind him, she resumed pacing the floor, sure she would never be able to sleep tonight. Everything in her life had turned to darkness. Fader had rejected her because she wanted to come to America to marry the man she loved. She stopped by the window and stared out, unseeing.

How could Olina love a man who could do that to her?

How could she turn off a love that had consumed most of her life? Here she was in a strange place where she couldn't even speak the language. Tomorrow she would board a train with the most insufferable man she had ever known.

Olina didn't remember Gustaf much from when they had been in Sweden. He was older than Lars and she, so he hadn't paid much attention to her, or she him. She never noticed him acting the way he was now.

Olina walked over and sat on the side of the bed. It had been so long since she slept in such a soft one. She had been looking forward to it, but with what had happened today, she didn't know if she would sleep a wink.

Olina didn't like to feel helpless, but that was what she felt right now. Helpless and alone. Alone and unloved. How much worse could it get? She didn't want to know. She wished she couldn't feel anything. That's what she could do. Stop feeling anything. Then maybe the hurt would go away.

Olina knew she could trust no one except herself. She would have to face this alone.

≈

Gustaf had been quiet at breakfast, and then he rushed her to Grand Central Station. What a large place it was! So fancy with arches and columns and all kinds of mosaic tiles. Olina had never seen anything like it. The ceiling seemed to be a million miles above them. People were everywhere, all talking in their own languages or the language of this new country. Occasionally, Olina heard a Swedish word as they made their way through the throng. It was like music to her ears, even though it was buried in the multilingual cacophony. The place was so large, they had barely made it to their train on time.

Olina was fighting a headache. The *clackity-clack* of the train was much louder than she had expected. Some people carried on conversations, which only added to the confusing din. She pressed her fingers to her temples as she tried to ignore all the noise.

This America was big. They had traveled for two days, and they hadn't reached Minnesota yet. At first Olina looked out the windows to see everything. . .and to keep from looking at Gustaf. Although she tried not to feel anything, every time she saw him, it brought all those feelings back; so she ignored him as much as she could.

There was a lot to see. Before they left the state of New York, Olina saw lots of trees—tall trees, many kinds that were new to her. As they traveled across other states, hills gave way to prairies with tall grasses blowing in the wind. Soon vast fields of wheat and other crops were interspersed with farm-houses and barns.

The train passed through small settlements as well as a few cities. It often stopped to let off and take on passengers. Soon the cities all looked a lot alike. They had crossed several states—Pennsylvania, Ohio, and Indiana—before they reached Chicago, Illinois, which was the largest city since they left New York City.

Every so often, she sat back and glanced at Gustaf in the seat facing hers. Every time she looked at him, Gustaf was reading the newspaper he bought in Grand Central Station. . . or he was asleep. . .or he was reading from his Bible, which he had in the carpetbag he carried. The only time he talked to her was when he needed to tell her something about the trip or when they were getting something to eat. That was fine with her.

Although Olina tried not to, she missed Lars. She also missed *Mor*. . .and her brothers. She could not even keep from missing Fader, even though he had hurt her so much. Maybe if she closed her eyes and rested her head against the back of the seat, her headache would go away.

&

Gustaf glanced up when he heard the soft breathy sound. Olina's head rested on the window beside her. Her eyes were closed, and her lips were slightly parted. She must be asleep, because the soft sounds that came from her small mouth were almost snores, but not quite. Gustaf wished he sat beside her. If he did, he would ease her head from the hard glass onto his softer broad shoulder. He would love to cushion her sleep there.

What was he thinking? He loved Anna, didn't he? The sweet honey smell of Olina had teased him when they were in the cab, but he had tried to ignore it.

Gustaf pulled his Bible out of his carpetbag again. His thoughts were not the thoughts of a man who planned to ask Anna to marry him the next time they were alone together. The sooner he got this mess with Olina fixed, the better for him. Gustaf leafed through the book, trying to find something that would ease his mind. But he went from one verse here to another verse there without gaining the peace he was seeking.

How had Olina gotten under his skin so much? Was it because he wanted to make up for what Lars did to hurt her? When she broke down and cried at the hotel, it touched Gustaf's heart. What he felt was pity, wasn't it? Then the next morning, Olina was somehow stronger. He had watched her, and he could see an iron will that kept her from showing the outside world how much she had been hurt. He admired that.

three

Would this train ride never end? The benches that had felt comfortable when they left New York were now almost too hard to bear. Olina squirmed, trying to find a softer spot, but to no avail. Most of her body was sore. She thought about Lars, and tears pooled in her eyes. When she thought about her family back in Sweden, the same thing happened. She would not cry. Crying didn't help anything. Olina wished she had something to read, but the newspaper Gustaf bought in New York City was in English. She couldn't read a word of it.

Olina's thoughts drifted to Tant Olga. What would she have done without her great-aunt?

About a year after Lars moved to America, Tant Olga asked if Olina would move into town to take care of her. At first Olina hadn't wanted to leave her beloved farm near the fjords. But she was glad when she did.

Tant Olga had fallen in love with a sailor when she was young. She married him against her family's wishes. *Farbror* Art had worked hard until he bought his own ship. As the wife of a merchant seaman, Tant Olga had enjoyed a life of plenty. Then her husband had been swept from the deck of his ship in a storm, leaving Tant Olga a wealthy woman. Art and Olga never had children of their own.

Tant Olga was an old woman when she asked Olina to live with her. She said she would pay Olina to take care of her. Olina had been worried that all she would do would be a drudge for Tant Olga. That had not been the case.

The two women, so far apart in age, were kindred spirits.

27

Tant Olga helped Olina become the woman she was today. Climbing the stairs in the three-story house and eating smaller portions of foods that weren't so rich helped Olina slim down. Tant Olga taught Olina to be a lady instead of a farm girl.

They enjoyed taking outings. The two of them even read the newspapers together, because they wanted to know what was going on in the world. Olina had written about these things in her letters to Lars. They discussed current events through their letters.

When Lars sent the money to come to America, Olina hadn't known what to do. Her father had forbidden her to go. But Tant Olga hadn't. When Tant Olga learned that her nephew opposed the trip, she assured Olina that he didn't mean it. She was convinced that when Olina asserted her independence and started on the journey, he would come to his senses and change his mind. Her father had changed his mind after she married Art. Olina hoped that would be the case with her own fader.

She didn't want to think about her father. She didn't want to cry again, so she pushed thoughts of him out of her head. Instead she returned to those days before her journey started.

Tant Olga helped her buy new clothes with the money she had saved. Tant Olga hadn't let Olina pay for anything she needed while she was staying with her, and she still paid her a wage for taking care of her. Over and over again, Olina told Tant Olga that she felt as though she were taking advantage of her, but Tant Olga didn't agree.

They studied the fashion books and bought the most popular fabrics. Tant Olga taught Olina how to sew and embroider and make lace. So when Olina made many of her clothes, they were the latest fashions, with extra touches. Tant Olga also helped her find a dressmaker who made other things for Olina when she was preparing for the journey to America.

Tant Olga even asked around until she found that Johanna

needed someone to go with her so she could join her husband in America. Without Tant Olga's help, Olina wouldn't be on this train somewhere in the interior of the vast country of America.

The train whistle cut through Olina's thoughts.

"This is our stop, Olina." Gustaf's words followed the sound. "Welcome to Litchfield, Minnesota."

Olina peeked out the window as the train slowed. The town of Litchfield spread on both sides of the tracks. It looked like many of the small towns they had come through on the long trip from New York City. Olina saw a mercantile and a livery stable near the tracks on one side. Other buildings surrounded them. One looked like a hotel. Even a building that appeared to be a saloon was nearby. On the other side of the tracks, the buildings looked more like homes. She saw a church steeple sticking up from a grove of trees that obscured much of that side of the town.

When the train came to a stop, Gustaf took Olina's hand to help her stand. Olina couldn't explain the funny feeling she had every time Gustaf touched her. Maybe it was because she had been traveling so long.

Olina stood poised on the platform and looked around. Beyond the depot, dirt streets were trimmed with wooden sidewalks. Hitching posts stood sentinel in front of various buildings, but they were different from the hitching posts in most of Europe. These were connected by a board. Many people were making use of both the sidewalks and the hitching posts. Single horses, horses with buggies, and horses with wagons were tied to several of the posts. Litchfield was a town full of life. Olina liked that.

As Olina continued her perusal of the town, she noticed that there were several stores down one street away from the depot. Maybe Litchfield was a larger town than she had first thought. She turned, looking for Gustaf. She spied him claiming her trunks from the baggage wagon. He pulled one up on his shoulders as if it didn't weigh much, but Olina knew better. She couldn't get the trunks down the stairs at Tant Olga's. The wagon driver helped bring them down when she was going to the ship.

Gustaf deposited the trunk beside the two carpetbags, which he had placed on a bench that ran the full length of the depot. Then he went back for the other. Olina walked over to stand beside the luggage.

"I'm going to leave you here to guard our bags." He didn't look at her while he was talking. Instead he looked around as if trying to see who was at the station. "I left my wagon at the livery. I'll go get it. You'll be safe waiting with our bags. I'll be back soon."

With long strides, he stepped off the station platform and marched to the livery. Olina sat beside the trunk. She was glad the bench was in the shade. The late morning sun was hotter than she thought it would be in April. Olina would be glad when they got to the Nilssons' farm. She could hardly wait to freshen up. And she wanted clean clothes. On the trip from New York City, she had changed her waist a couple of times with fresh waists she had packed in her carpetbag. But she had worn these clothes too long.

What she actually needed was a bath. She would love to soak in a bathtub, such as Tant Olga had in her upstairs bathroom, filled with tepid water. One like she used in the hotel in New York City. She needed to wash her hair. It felt as if it were sticking to her scalp. They couldn't get to the farm any too soon for her.

When Olina heard a wagon pull up beside the platform, she turned to see if it was Gustaf. It was, but he didn't look happy.

"I'm afraid we're not going straight to the farm. Mother sent a list to August at the livery, asking that I pick some things up at the mercantile. I hope that doesn't inconvenience you."

Why did he sound so formal? It made Olina uncomfortable. "No, that'll be just fine, for sure."

Gustaf helped her up from the bench, then took her arm and lifted her into the wagon. While she was busy arranging her skirt on the seat, Gustaf crossed in front of the team of matched black horses. He took time to whisper to the horses and caress their faces before he climbed into the wagon. The seat was wide, but Gustaf was a big man. His presence beside her seemed to crowd Olina.

"Just wait here," Gustaf said as he stopped the wagon in front of a store that was about a block from the train station. "I'll be right back." Gustaf stepped down and tied the horses to the hitching post.

At least he had parked in the shade. Olina was still hotter than she wanted to be. She glanced into the open door of the store. It looked cool inside. What could it hurt if she moved out of the heat?

With that thought, Olina clambered down from the wagon and stepped into the cool interior of the store. What a lot of merchandise they carried. Why, she could probably get anything she would ever need right here. Olina noticed a display of fabrics on a far wall. She made her way through the crowded store and started feeling the texture of various pieces.

A soft feminine voice sounded behind Olina. Olina turned and glanced at the blond girl who stood there. Then she moved as close to the fabric as she could. She had not understood what the young woman said. She guessed that she might want to get by.

"Olina Sandstrom?" Now the voice was excited.

Olina looked once again. "Were you talking to me?" she asked in Swedish.

"Ja," the girl answered and continued in Swedish. "Don't you know me? It's Merta Petersson. We used to live near you."

"Of course." Olina reached to hug the girl. Finally someone she knew and who spoke the same language she did. "But I would have never known you. How old were we when you moved? Seven or eight? You've really changed, for sure."

"You have, too." Merta nodded. "But I would recognize you anywhere. You always had the most beautiful eyes."

Olina blushed at the compliment. "Do you live here in Litchfield?"

"I do now. Until last week, I lived on a farm with my family, but I got married." Now Merta was blushing. "How did you get here?" Merta looked around the store to see who was there. "Who are you with?"

"I'm with Gustaf Nilsson." Olina couldn't help wondering if Merta knew that Lars sent her the money to come to America, but she didn't want to ask her, in case she didn't. She also wondered if Merta knew about Lars's marriage. Gustaf had indicated that the family had just found out about it. Maybe no one else in town knew yet.

"Yes. I saw his wagon outside," Merta said. "I'm so glad you are visiting here. I hope we can spend some time together before you go home."

"I'm sure we can." Olina noticed Gustaf heading toward the door. "I would like that," she added before turning and following him out the door.

four

Gustaf started the horses moving toward the edge of town. Olina had a lot to think about. Merta was married now.

She didn't even tell me what her married name was. Maybe Gustaf knows.

"Did you see Merta in the store?" she asked as she turned her gaze toward him.

"Yes."

"She told me she was married, but she didn't tell me her married name."

"It's Swenson." The curt answer spurted from Gustaf's stiff lips.

What's wrong with him now? Is he always in a bad mood?

Olina hoped the farm wasn't too far from town. She was ready to talk to someone besides this sullen man. She took a deep breath to keep from sighing. How easy it would be to give in to the desolation that threatened to engulf her. At this moment, she had no one to depend on. No matter what awaited her at the farm, she would take care of herself.

Olina didn't know what the rest of the Nilsson family thought about what had happened. She wasn't even sure what Gustaf thought about it. Except he called her a mess that had to be cleaned up. He said he would take care of her, but she didn't want him taking care of her.

Olina liked this Minnesota. Although the land was flat with a few small rolling hills, it was beautiful. Tall green prairie grass blew in the gentle breeze. Dotted over the green were patches of prairie flowers. Some were white, some pink or yellow. Olina wondered what they were called. They were unlike any flowers she had seen in Sweden. No wonder everything looked so green. She often caught glimpses of water shining through the grass. The farms they passed had many of their fields in cultivation, covered with bright green shoots of some kind.

When they first left town, Olina asked a few questions, but Gustaf answered in monosyllables. Soon she gave up.

❧

After the few attempts at conversation, Gustaf also rode quietly, thinking his own thoughts. He didn't point out the beautiful wild flowers, or the small lakes, or even the road to their neighbor's farm. He sat berating himself. Maybe if he had made Lars face his own mistakes, he would have learned to be more responsible.

He couldn't even imagine what Olina must be going through, but he was beginning to admire her. He wished he could be more help to her; but whenever he thought about the last few days, anger still boiled up inside him. He didn't know who he was the angriest at, Lars or himself.

When they reached the farm, decisions had to be made about Olina. Would he have any say in what happened? He hoped that he would. He wanted to help this young woman who shared the wagon seat with him, so close that he could feel her even though they were not touching. He wanted to help her. Occasionally on the train, he caught a glimpse of the hurt that lingered deep within her. What could he have done to help prevent it?

❧

"Our farm starts right here." Gustaf pointed toward the fence line that divided the land on their right.

The sound of his voice, after riding so far without talking, startled Olina. She jerked, then turned to look where he was pointing.

"It's still a ways before we come to the drive up to the house."

How could Gustaf sound as if everything were normal? Maybe he was right. Soon she would face the whole Nilsson family. She didn't want to fall apart the first time someone spoke to her.

"The crops look good." Olina was surprised that her voice didn't tremble. "What is growing in that field?"

"This one has winter wheat," Gustaf answered. "We'll plant corn in the next field, though."

Olina didn't think she had ever seen corn growing. She wondered if she would be here to see it.

"Just past that field, we'll turn in and head toward the house."

Olina gazed over the fields toward a grove of trees growing back from the road. "Is the house up there among the trees?"

"Yes. We bought the farm from Ben Johnson's widow. They had been on the farm for a long time. He was the one who built the house. The trees keep it cool in the summertime and protect it from some of the harsh winds in the winter."

Olina tried to see the house from where they were, but it was too far away. "Why did Mrs. Johnson sell such a wonderful farm?" Olina turned to look at Gustaf.

"They didn't have children, and she was getting older. She couldn't run the farm by herself."

"Couldn't she hire someone to help her?"

"Yes, but she felt alone when Mr. Johnson died. She wanted to move back East with her sister. It was our good luck that she was ready to sell about the time we got here. No one else tried to buy it. It's a big farm, so it cost quite a lot. After we sold everything we had in Sweden to come to Minnesota, we had enough money to buy it from her."

Gustaf turned the horses down a long drive bordered on one

side by a plowed field and on the other side by another field of wheat. "She didn't want to move all of her furniture across the country. I think her sister had married a wealthy merchant in some city back east. She already had a nice house full of furniture. We were able to move in and live right away. Of course, over time, Mother has made the house into her own home."

When Gustaf chuckled at that, Olina was able to laugh along with him, at least a little. She remembered how homey Ingrid Nilsson's house always was. How happy it made Ingrid and her family.

❧

It was a little laugh, but Gustaf felt part of the heavy weight he had been carrying slip with the sound of it.

Maybe, just maybe, Olina will be able to get over what Lars has done to her. And maybe someday she will forgive me.

five

Gerda Nilsson must have heard the wagon coming up the long drive to the house, because she rushed out onto the porch. Olina was glad to see the friend she had grown up with. But the young woman standing on the porch was no longer the girl who had romped through the meadows with her. Gerda's hair was up in the new pompadour style that was coming into fashion. The pouf formed a soft blond halo that framed her delicate features, features that were so like the ones Olina remembered, and yet so different. But then, they both were.

As Olina climbed down from the wagon seat, her gaze was drawn to the two-story farmhouse so different from the houses she was used to seeing in Sweden. Farmhouses back home were usually only one story. Instead of rock that was used over there, this American home was built of wood and painted white. Dark green shutters framed the windows on both the lower story and the upper story. Porches at home were small, but this house had a covered porch that spread along the lower story, covering at least three-fourths of it. White columns supported the roof of the porch, and a railing connected the columns except where steps led up to the porch.

Olina thought it must be wonderful to sit in the inviting rocking chairs that were scattered the length of it. Three sat on either side of the front door. The house looked enormous to Olina, much larger than farmhouses in Sweden.

"Olina!" Gerda rushed down the steps.

"Gerda!" Olina scrambled over the side of the wagon,

catching her foot in the hem of her skirt. She would have fallen if strong hands hadn't caught her. She didn't want to look at Gustaf. He might be able to see how much his touch affected her, even though she didn't want it to. Her emotions were too close to the surface.

Gerda threw her arms around Olina and held her as if she would never let go. "I'm so glad you're here. I've missed you so much." She sounded as if she were about to cry.

Maybe she would think that Olina was only emotional about seeing her. "I've missed you, too. It seems like forever since you left."

When the two girls finally pulled apart, tears were streaming down their faces. Gerda pulled a handkerchief from the pocket of her apron and gently wiped Olina's face. Then she dried her own tears.

Gerda took Olina by the arm and drew her toward the porch. Flower beds spread in front, and young plants were beginning to bud. There were even a few rose bushes. Olina had always loved the smell of roses. She doubted that she would be here when the buds opened enough to share their delightful fragrance.

"Mor has just left to take dinner to *Far* and the hired men, but she left food in case you got here before she returned. She wanted to be here when you arrived, but the men have to be fed. I was glad she let me stay at the house and wait for you." Gerda opened the door that led into the formal parlor.

Gustaf followed them in, carrying Olina's smaller bag.

Olina liked the furniture, upholstered in wine-colored velvet. It was different from what she was used to in Sweden, but it was attractive. A thick carpet spread to within a foot of each wall. Even Tant Olga's house didn't have carpet. Everything matched so well, not like the hodgepodge of furniture her family had collected over the years. Lace curtains and doilies knitted the decor together. Mor would love to see this beautiful place.

"What room do you want Olina to have?" Gustaf was heading toward the hall that was behind the parlor.

"I wanted her to share mine, so we could really catch up." Gerda glanced at Olina before she continued, "But Mor said we should give her the bedroom on the front corner. That way she can have her privacy, but we'll still spend time together when we want to."

Gustaf nodded and ducked through the doorway. In the hallway outside the parlor was the stairway. He climbed up the steep stairs as if they were level ground. Olina followed him at a slower pace.

"When you've freshened up, come down to eat." Gerda stood looking up after her friend. "I put fresh water in your room."

⋅⋆⋅

Olina met Gustaf as he came from the bedroom that would be hers. His presence made the narrow hall feel even narrower. Olina needed to have more room between them. Why did his presence unsettle her? He was like all the other men in her life. He didn't want her, but she felt drawn to him even though she wanted to push him away. She felt as if the dark hall did not have enough air. She was having a hard time taking a breath.

"I can wait to bring up your trunks." Gustaf looked down at her. "That way you'll have plenty of time to freshen up."

"What I really need"—Olina moved toward the beckoning doorway—"is a long, soaking bath. It feels as though it's been a lifetime since we were in New York."

"Wouldn't you like to eat first?"

Olina slowly nodded.

Gustaf pointed to another door halfway down the hallway. "That's the bathroom. We have a large tub in there. A man from Norway invented an automatic storage water heater a few years ago, and we've just installed one, so we don't have to carry hot water upstairs for the bathtub."

Again Olina nodded. Then she stepped into the bedroom that would be hers for awhile. How long, she could only guess. She was going to have to make some decisions, but she didn't want to think about them right now. She pulled out her hat pin and removed her hat. Dropping her hat on the table by the bed, she walked over and looked out the window that faced the front of the house. There was another window on the side of the house, and a gentle breeze blew through the room. More lace curtains covered these windows, and matching lace draped across the bed. How inviting that bed looked. Maybe she should lie down and forget everything. But she couldn't. It was there in her heart. . .in her mind. . .in every part of her.

After picking up the pitcher of water, she poured some into the matching bowl. Both of them were decorated with hand-painted roses. As she splashed the water on her face, its coolness soothed her. Gerda must have filled the pitcher right before they arrived.

Taking off the jacket of her traveling suit, she looked down at her wilted, dusty white waist. It didn't matter. Gerda and Gustaf had already seen it. She decided not to change until after her bath. Olina picked up the rose-scented soap and washed her hands. She dried her face and hands with the embroidered linen towel that lay on the washstand beside the pitcher and bowl. How was she ever going to get through the evening? She crossed the hardwood floor and descended the stairs, trying to rein in her emotions.

Gerda and Gustaf kept the conversation light and informative as they all ate homemade bread and ham, accompanied by applesauce that Gerda and her mother canned last autumn. Olina learned a lot about the farm, the neighbors, and the many activities that occurred in the close-knit community.

Although they were a ways from town, many of the neighbors were from Norway or Sweden, and they often got together. Women visited over tea or held quilting bees as well as other bees. They had helped Merta Swenson make her linens before her marriage. It sounded like a lot of fun, but Olina wondered if she would ever have fun again. Men helped each other harvest crops, build barns, or mend broken farming equipment. But no one could help fix her broken heart.

They had even established a school close by. The school building was also used to hold church services when the weather was too bad to get into town. Olina would have loved getting married here and establishing her family in this community. Now there would not be any family. At least not for Olina and Lars.

And who else was there? Unbidden, a face swam into Olina's mind. A face so like Lars, only more mature. A face with icy blue eyes, but she had seen those eyes warm when he had looked at his sister. Why was she thinking about Gustaf? He was nothing to her. Nothing but her best friend's brother.

Olina needed to make a decision. What was she going to do? What could she do? She had very little money. Not enough to go back to Sweden. The only thing she could do was write her father and beg his forgiveness for going against his wishes. If he forgave her, maybe he would send her the money to come home. That is, if he had enough money to send.

Olina was soaking in a tub of warm water when she heard Mrs. Nilsson return. The sound of voices rumbled below her, but she couldn't make out what they were saying. She did recognize their voices as both Gerda and Gustaf talked to their mother. Was their conversation about her? Soon the talking ceased, and Olina heard Gerda and Gustaf leave the house.

Tears streamed down Olina's face and plopped in the cooling bath water. She felt chilled, inside and out. She got out of the bathtub and pulled the plug. As the water gurgled down the drain, Olina dried off and put on fresh clothes. At least she felt better being clean again. Tonight, when she was once more alone in her room, she would write her father a letter.

ఈ

Mrs. Nilsson was waiting in the kitchen for Olina when she came down the stairs. She opened her arms and gathered Olina close.

"My precious child." There was a catch in her voice. "I'm sorry that my son treated you so wrong." By the end of the second sentence, both Olina and Mrs. Nilsson were crying.

Olina quickly regained her composure and pulled out of the embrace. She reached for the handkerchief she had earlier stuffed into her sleeve. After wiping her face, she turned toward the woman she once thought would be her mother-in-law.

Mrs. Nilsson was also wiping tears from her cheeks. "Since we received the letter, I have asked myself if I did something wrong when I was rearing Lars. How could my son have done something so irresponsible and hurtful?"

"For sure, it's not your fault that this has happened," Olina said. "But I don't know what I'm going to do now."

Mrs. Nilsson pulled a chair out from the table for Olina. "After supper tonight, we'll have a talk with Bennel. He'll know what we should do."

ఈ

Evidently Gustaf had gone out to help Mr. Nilsson in the fields, because they both came in for the evening meal at the same time. Mr. Nilsson didn't say anything about Lars to Olina before they ate, but when the meal was over, he asked Olina and Mrs. Nilsson to accompany him into the parlor. Gustaf followed them. Evidently his fader didn't mind, because he didn't tell him to go away.

Mr. Nilsson indicated that Olina should sit on the sofa

beside his wife. Mrs. Nilsson took Olina's hand and squeezed it. Olina knew she was trying to make Olina relax, but she couldn't. Maybe it was because of what her fader had done to her. Mr. Nilsson felt too much like her fader. The stern expression on his face caused her to be nervous.

"First, Olina, I want to apologize to you for what my son did. I can imagine that you are extremely hurt."

Olina could tell that he meant what he said. She nodded.

The expression on Mr. Nilsson's face softened. "I can never make up for what Lars did, but I want you to know that we love you as if you were our own daughter. You have a home here as long as you want one."

"Thank you." It was hard for Olina to get the words out because her throat was dry.

"We'll do anything we can to help you." Mr. Nilsson got up from the chair where he was sitting and stood beside his wife, placing his hand on her shoulder. "While you are in our home, we hope you'll think of us as your parents."

Olina bowed her head a moment before she raised it and answered. "Thank you. I'd like that."

Mrs. Nilsson patted Olina's hand, which rested on the sofa between them. "Do you have any plans for now?"

"Well, I don't have the money to go back to Sweden." Olina tried to swallow the lump that had come in her throat. "I plan to write Fader a letter tonight, asking him to help me come home." Olina couldn't tell them what her father had said before she left Sweden. She hoped she never would have to tell anyone.

Gustaf didn't say anything while this conversation was going on, but Olina could feel his gaze on her. She glanced and caught an expression on his face that she had never seen before. It made her feel as if he cared what happened to her, not at all like the man in New York City who called her a mess.

six

Olina wondered how long she would have to wait for an answer to her letter. Knowing it would take a long time, she tried to hide her hurt from the members of the Nilsson family. She thought she was doing it quite well. However, after only a few of days, Gerda came to her room a little while before supper.

"Olina." Gerda sat on the side of Olina's bed and watched her friend as she fussed with her hair. "I haven't wanted to pry. I wanted to wait until you shared with me, but you haven't." Gerda got up and went to stand behind Olina, looking directly into the reflection of her face in the mirror. "It's hard for me to watch you hurting so badly. We've been friends a long time. Can't you let me help you?"

Olina turned from the mirror and walked over to the window. She pulled back the curtain that gently blew in the breeze, trying to find something to fix her gaze on. Although her focus wandered from the birds in the trees, to the open barn door, to the sparkle of water barely visible beyond the roof of the barn, none of these things interested her. She paused a minute before answering, trying to decide how much to tell Gerda. Then she turned to face her dear friend.

"Oh, Gerda." A shuddering breath shook her frame. "I haven't known what to say. . .or if I could say anything without crying." The sentence ended with a soft sob.

Gerda pulled Olina into her arms and hugged her, gently rubbing her back as she broke into sobs muffled against Gerda's soft calico dress. The soothing touch brought comfort

44

to Olina. It had been too long since someone who loved her had held her. She missed her mother's touch. Tant Olga had hugged her occasionally, too.

When Olina stopped crying, she pulled away and swiped, with both hands, at the tears on her face. Gerda picked up a soft white handkerchief and helped Olina mop away the moisture that had completely covered her face and soaked the shoulder of Gerda's dress.

"Oh my, I must look a fright." Olina turned toward the oval mirror on the wall. "My face is all puffy and red." She patted some hairs into place before turning back toward Gerda. "I don't think I'll have any supper tonight. I'm not really hungry." She didn't want anyone else in the family to see her like this.

Gerda gazed deep into her eyes before turning toward the door. "I know you helped feed the chickens and gather the eggs. And you insisted on hanging the clothes on the line for Mother. That's enough to work up an appetite. I'll make both of us sandwiches out of cold roast beef and cheese. We'll grab an apple apiece and go down to the creek for a picnic supper."

Olina had no answer for her, except to nod. After Gerda left, Olina glanced down at her white blouse that had become soiled when she was gathering the eggs. While Gerda went down to fix their supper, she changed into a soft green calico. Looking at the white collar and cuffs trimmed with lace that she usually wore with the dress, she decided to leave them off. She was glad that she had plaited her hair and wound it around her head that morning. It was suitable for a picnic on the banks of a stream.

After tramping down the fencerow of a large field, the two girls ambled out across a pasture toward the grove of trees that lined the banks of the stream. Each girl carried her supper in a small tin lard bucket. Gerda told her that they were the ones the Nilsson children had used when they were younger to carry their lunches to school. It made Olina feel young and almost carefree. But not completely. She could not bury her hurt that deep.

The day had been warm for late spring, and it was a long walk. Both girls began to perspire before they entered the cool shadows of the trees. Taking a well-worn path through the underbrush, they soon arrived at the bank of the flowing water. A small sandbar led from the verdant growth to the stream, and a few large stones jutted out into the water. One even formed a flat shelf above the flow.

Gerda walked out on the stone shelf that was still warm from the sun, although it was now shaded from the branches of the trees that hung over it. Olina followed her, watching bubbles and gurgles burst from the water as it swirled around the rocks. Gerda sat cross-legged on the rock and arranged her skirt to cover her legs. Then she put her lard bucket in her lap. After prying off the lid with a stick she had picked up as they walked through the woods, Gerda pulled out a sandwich wrapped in paper.

Olina did the same. Before she laid her sandwich on the full skirt that spread around her on the rock, she took a bite. It tasted heavenly. Olina hadn't realized how hungry she really was. After taking another bite, she looked back into the bucket. It contained more than just an apple. She pulled out another lump of paper and unrolled a sweet pickle. When Olina sank her teeth into it, pickle juice dripped down her chin. She reached up with her free hand, trying to catch it before it stained her dress.

"This tastes good." Olina wiped her mouth on a napkin that was also in her bucket.

"Mother and I made those last summer." Gerda unwrapped her own pickle. "It's a recipe Anna Jenson gave us. We all like it, especially Gustaf." Gerda took a bite of her sandwich. After she finished chewing it, she said, "Of course, Gustaf likes everything Anna makes."

Olina looked up. "Is she a wonderful cook?" She didn't know why she was so interested, but she was.

"Oh, she's a good cook," Gerda answered, "but I think Gustaf would like it even if it wasn't that good. He likes everything about Anna. The whole family expects them to marry sometime soon."

Olina didn't know why that should bother her, but it did. She looked up at Gerda, who was now digging other packages out of her bucket. "Why did you say that?"

Gerda looked up. "Say what?"

"That the family expects them to marry. Has he asked her to marry him?"

Gerda went back to unwrapping her supper. "I don't think so. She would have told us. . .or he would have. They're together a lot. I think he's calling on her."

Olina nodded even though Gerda wasn't looking. She took a bite of the sandwich again, and what had tasted heavenly a few minutes ago now turned to sand in her mouth, making her throat dry. She looked around for something to dip the water with.

Gerda dipped her empty bucket into the cool, moving water and handed it to Olina. "Drink this. You look as though you need it right now."

Olina turned the bucket up and gulped the soothing water, dripping some down the front of her dress. Then she emptied her own bucket of food and handed it to Gerda. "Here you can use mine."

The rest of the meal was eaten in silence by the two girls. Olina tried to force the food past the large lump in her throat. At any other time, the sandwich, pickle, chocolate cake, and apple would have tasted good. But not tonight. They were only so much sawdust to chew and wash down with lots of water. She was glad when all the packages were empty. She hadn't wanted to hurt Gerda by not finishing what she had fixed for them.

When Gerda was through with her food, she pulled off her shoes and stockings and dangled her feet into the water. "Are you ever going to talk to me? I know Lars hurt you, and I know that Gustaf didn't tell you about it as soon as he should have. But I thought we were best friends. I want to help you if I can."

Olina followed Gerda's lead and soon splashed her feet in the refreshing stream. As they sat there, Olina did reveal part of her heart to her friend. They discussed Lars and how he had hurt her and how Gustaf had treated her in New York City and on the trip to Minnesota. But Olina couldn't tell her friend about her own father rejecting her. Or that she no longer felt she could trust God.

੩੪

Since it was such a warm spring day, Gustaf soon worked up a sweat. He loaded the wagon full of hay and took it to the pasture where the dairy cattle were kept. There he scattered the hay into four piles in different parts of the pasture, helping supplement the meager grass. Then he plowed the only field that hadn't been done before he went to New York. All the time he was following the horses pulling the large implement, he thought about that fateful journey, his anger on the trip there, and his confusion on the journey back.

It wasn't long before his thoughts settled on Olina. He would never be able to remove some images from his memory. Olina as she stood on the dock waiting for Lars. Olina at dinner at the hotel. Olina in the hall of the hotel when he had blurted out the truth about Lars. How different Olina was the next morning. She had strength and poise.

He couldn't understand what it was about her that drew

him. But something did. Olina filled his thoughts as Anna never had. He couldn't remember thinking about Anna so much while he was working. He had a hard time concentrating on making the rows straight while his thoughts were in captivity to Olina.

What was he going to do? He knew that everyone, including Anna and his family, expected him to ask Anna to marry him. He wasn't sure he could do that now. How could he hurt her that way? Anna had meant a lot to him for a long time. But did he love her enough to marry her? That was a question he would have to answer soon. When he tried to bring her image to mind, Olina's face sometimes took its place. A lot of good his thoughts of Olina were. She didn't trust him, and he didn't know if she ever would. How could he have said those things to her in New York? What had he been thinking?

Gustaf didn't know what he was going to do. He knew that what he already felt for Olina was a major impediment to his stagnant relationship with Anna.

Gustaf worked even harder trying to clear the thoughts from his mind, but they wouldn't leave. He was glad when he finished the last row of the field. After unhitching the plow, he drove the horses into the barn before removing their harness. While he rubbed them down, he decided to go to the creek to take a swim before supper.

Because his mind was on other things, he didn't notice that the prairie grass, on the way to the grove of trees, was trampled down. It never entered his mind that someone had beaten him to the quiet haven.

As Gustaf walked the path through the underbrush, he pulled down his suspenders. Then he stripped off the sweat-soaked shirt and threw it onto a bush near the end of the path. He had started unbuttoning his trousers when he emerged from the woods and first heard the soft murmur of feminine voices. Startled, he froze just as Olina turned her eyes toward the rustle he made coming through the brush.

Shock registered on her face as her gaze swept from his unbuttoned waistband across his naked chest to his face. Blood rushed to color her cheeks, and she swiftly looked away.

Gustaf's first inclination was to cover up, but his shirt was nowhere near him. So he dove into the deep swimming hole formed by a small cove on the creek. He didn't even take time to remove his work boots. He was thankful that the creek wasn't over his head there because his heavy boots pulled his feet to the bottom, and he stood chest high in the water.

"Gustaf, what are you doing here?" Gerda started gathering up the scattered papers and putting them in her bucket. "We didn't know you were coming for a swim."

"I didn't know you were here, either." Gustaf pushed his wet hair back over his head.

"Is that why you went in swimming with your boots on?" Gerda covered her mouth to hide a giggle.

Gustaf looked down into the clear water. "Well, so I have. No wonder I'm having trouble swimming." He burst out laughing. The sound reverberated from the rocks and trees that surrounded them.

Gustaf noticed that Olina was laughing, too. A high musical sound. It was wonderful to hear. Before they had left Sweden, she had been a happy, fun-loving girl. He had often heard her laugh peal across the fields as she and Lars, or she and Gerda, were playing. He hadn't realized how much he had missed the sound of it until it wafted across the water to him. Maybe his being all wet was a good thing if it could start her laughing again.

Gerda and Olina both pulled their feet from the water and picked up their shoes and stockings. After looping their buckets over their arms, they started back toward the path.

"We'll let you swim in peace." Gerda smiled at her brother before following Olina through the opening in the bushes.

As they walked away, Gustaf could hear them giggling as if they were little girls. He was sure they were discussing him, but that was all right. Olina was laughing again.

❧

The day after they washed the clothes, Mrs. Nilsson wanted to wash all the sheets and towels. Olina was glad to help her. While the water was heating, she went upstairs and started taking all the sheets off the beds. She made a pile in the hall at the top of the stairs. When she finished in the last bedroom, she spread out one of the sheets and placed the others on it. After pulling the corners together, she tied them in a soft knot and picked them up to carry downstairs. It was hard to see around the large bundle, and her mind was on her problem.

When Olina had gone down about half of the steep stairs, her foot slipped, and she was unable to regain her balance. Her elbow struck one of the stairs, and a pain shot up and down that arm. She shut her eyes and groaned as she hit another step.

Something stopped her descent, and a concerned voice sounded near her ear. "Olina, are you all right?"

Olina opened her eyes and stared up into Gustaf's face, which was very near hers. "I think so."

She lost her precarious hold on the bundle, and it fell to the bottom of the stairs. Gustaf eased himself down on the step beside Olina. He reached up and wiped a tear that had made its way down her cheek.

"You're crying. Are you sure you're not hurt?"

Olina rubbed the elbow and couldn't keep from wincing. It did hurt. "I hit my elbow on the stairs."

Gustaf carefully assisted her to stand. "Is that all that hurts?"

"I think so."

"Can you walk?"

Olina nodded.

Gustaf helped her the rest of the way down the stairs. He took her into the kitchen and pulled out a chair. "Sit here. Let me look at your elbow."

His touch was gentle as his fingers probed the area. "I think your arm is swelling."

He went to the sink and dipped a towel into cool water. When he came back, he made a pad with the wet cloth and tied another around it to keep it on her arm.

Olina watched all these ministrations with interest. This man was different from the man who met her in New York City. She would have never thought that Gustaf could be so caring, especially to her.

"Thank you." Olina started to get up.

His hand on her shoulder kept her in the chair. "You need to sit here and let the cool water ease your pain."

"But your moder is waiting for me to bring her the sheets to wash."

Gustaf glanced to the bundle that lay in a heap in the hall between the kitchen and the parlor. "I'll take them to her. She would want you to take care of yourself."

Olina watched in amazement as Gustaf hefted the bundle onto his shoulder as if it were as light as a feather and carried it out the back door. Maybe she should rethink her opinion of him.

 largeroman

Gustaf wasn't sure why he went into the house at that moment, but when he saw Olina's foot slip, his heart jumped into his throat. He rushed to stop her from tumbling all the way to the bottom of the stairs. She would have hurt more than her elbow if that had happened. Something deep inside him reached out to her. It wasn't just her beauty that called to him.

Olina had faced her terrible dilemma with more strength than most men would have had in the same circumstances. He admired the way she fit right into the family, sharing the workload with Mor and Gerda. Of course, she was kind of quiet when the family was all together, but he was sure she had a lot to think about. It would be awhile before she had an answer from her father. Gustaf hoped that when it came, Olina's troubles would be over. But something within him didn't want her to leave Minnesota.

❧

After supper, the family went into the parlor. Mrs. Nilsson picked up her knitting, and Mr. Nilsson read to the family from the newspaper he had picked up in town. Gerda and Olina sat on the sofa. Gustaf sat on the floor beside it.

"How is your arm, Olina?" he asked when his father stopped reading out loud.

She looked down at his upturned face. "It's much better."

"I'm glad."

Mr. Nilsson folded up the newspaper and laid it on the table beside his chair. "What happened to Olina?" He sounded compassionate.

"She was helping me," Mrs. Nilsson told him, "and she fell on the stairs."

"But Gustaf stopped me from going all the way down." She turned back to Gustaf. "I didn't thank you, did I?"

This was the first time Olina really took part in the conversation. She felt more comfortable and a part of the family.

The next day, Olina was helping Mrs. Nilsson once again. Several times during the day, Gustaf came by wherever she was and spent a few minutes talking to her. Soon this became a daily habit. The friendship continued to develop, but Olina wanted to be careful. Of course, it was just a friendship. Gustaf was spoken for, wasn't he?

seven

Olina had been in Minnesota for three weeks. The Nilsson family planned a party to introduce her to the neighbors. Olina dreaded that celebration. She didn't know how she could face all the people when they found out that she had come to America to marry Lars. Maybe if she had a headache or stomachache or something, she wouldn't have to go. Everyone else could enjoy the gathering whether she was there or not. Then she found out that the doctor was coming. If she pretended to be sick, Mrs. Nilsson would have him look at her. He would surely know that nothing was wrong with her.

Things had gotten better since the day she and Gerda had the picnic. Maybe she could make it through the party. If things got tough, she could remember how Gustaf looked when he jumped into the water, the way the cool stream had darkened his white blond hair to a honey color. But that memory also recalled his broad muscular chest liberally sprinkled with blond hairs. With that picture came feelings that Olina didn't understand, a tightness deep within her that she had never felt before. It made her feel breathless. She had to remind herself that she didn't trust men. Besides, Gustaf was promised to Anna, wasn't he?

At least the party would bring one good thing. She would finally get to see this Anna. What would she look like? She wondered if Anna was prettier than she was. What did it matter? She didn't mean anything special to Gustaf, and he wasn't special to her. Was he?

❧

The schoolhouse looked festive when Olina and Gerda walked

54

in. Whenever there was a party, the whole farming community helped. Chains made from colored paper draped around the rafters, and lanterns hung on hooks all around the walls. The young women were drawn toward long tables made from lumber laid across sawhorses and covered with tablecloths in various colors. Holding down the cloths were fancy dishes containing all kinds of goodies. Everyone must have brought their most cherished glass plates and bowls. Cakes and pastries took up half of one table.

Olina loved pastry, especially *munk*. The fried pieces of slightly sweet dough were especially good when they were rolled in sugar as soon as they came from the kettle. She could even see that one plate held *äppelmunk*, tasty doughnuts filled with apples and cinnamon before they were fried. She couldn't identify all of the kinds of cake, but she did see *gräddbakelse*. This cream cake was a favorite of hers. Olina knew she would have to be careful not to eat too much or she would look just as she had when she first went to live with Tant Olga.

Every one of the neighbor women had fixed several of their best recipes for the party. Olina decided that a large crowd must be coming to eat that much food.

"How many people will be here tonight?" she asked Gerda as they hung their shawls on two of the empty hooks on the wall near the door.

Turning around, Gerda looked across the group that already filled the room. "Everyone is here." Then she looked again. "But I don't see Anna. The Jensons are late as usual. I think Anna likes to make an entrance."

The two friends walked over to the table where Mrs. Nilsson was pouring apple cider into a variety of cups. "Here, Olina." Gerda handed her a cup before she took one for herself. "Mrs. Swenson, Merta's mother-in-law, makes the best cider."

Just as Olina reached for the proffered beverage, a large

family came through the door accompanied by a lot of noise.

"There are the Jensons." Gerda took a slow sip of cider. "The one with the dark hair is Anna."

Olina was surprised. Anna Jenson was pretty enough, with bright eyes and a smiling face, but she stood tall and sturdy. Olina could tell by looking at her that she was a hard worker and strong. Her upswept hair braided and looped into a figure-eight bun low on the back of her head. Her laugh, though infectious, was a little too loud.

Olina looked around for Gustaf. She was surprised that he hadn't gone to greet his intended. If Olina were promised to someone, she would want him by her side at a party, especially one given to introduce a new girl to the community. Now why was she thinking about that? It didn't matter to her what kind of relationship Anna and Gustaf had, did it?

The night was a great success. Olina enjoyed meeting the neighbors, and they welcomed her with open arms. Some of the neighbors had emigrated from the same area where she had lived in Sweden. She renewed acquaintances with them. After inquiring about her family, they moved on to asking her how she liked Minnesota. No one wondered why she came, so she soon relaxed and enjoyed herself, pushing to the back of her mind and heart the fact that she was still hurting. She needed to get on with her life. Maybe soon her visit would be over, after her reply from her father arrived.

≥≥

When Anna and her family came in the door, Gustaf started to go to her, but his attention was drawn to Olina, where she stood by Gerda, drinking cider. He couldn't keep from comparing the two women.

Anna was familiar and comfortable. Olina caused something inside Gustaf to tug his heart. The last week or so, their friendship had grown, and he liked that. But would a man who intended to marry one woman develop such a strong friendship with another? Of course not. He knew he couldn't pursue the feelings Olina caused until he talked to Anna. He would wait until the end of the evening and ask if he could drive her home. Gustaf didn't want her hurt at the party, and what he needed to say to her would be upsetting. He knew that if he loved her as a husband should love his wife, he wouldn't be so interested in Olina. Anna deserved more than that from the man she would marry.

❧

During the evening, Gerda or her mother made sure Olina met everyone in attendance. When the dancing started, accompanied by a fiddle and an accordion, playing some American music and some Scandinavian music, Olina was never without a partner. All the young men, and even some of the older men, asked her to dance. All the men except Gustaf.

That Gustaf didn't dance with her shouldn't have mattered, but it did. Why did he stay so far away from her? Olina watched him covertly all through the evening. He didn't dance with Anna any more often than he did with the other young women. Maybe Gerda was wrong. Maybe there wasn't an understanding between them. And what difference did that make to her? Nothing. Not any difference at all.

However, several hours later while the women were gathering up their nearly empty dishes, Olina noticed Gustaf talking earnestly with Anna. Anna stood smiling up at him. Although Anna was a tall woman, he was several inches taller. After a moment, they walked together to the hooks along the back wall. Gustaf took a long blue cape off one hook and draped it around Anna's shoulders. Then they left together.

A dull ache started in Olina's heart. Trying to hide it, she helped Mrs. Nilsson gather up all the things they had brought.

"Where is a broom?" Olina asked as she put the last table-cloth in the basket. "I'll sweep the floor. Most everyone is gone."

"Oh no, you won't." Gerda took the basket from her hands and started out the door to take it to the wagon. "You were the guest of honor. You won't be cleaning up," she called back over her shoulder.

"It's all right." Mrs. Nilsson was standing beside Olina now. "Tomorrow Gerda and Merta will come and clean up the schoolhouse. No one wants to stay tonight, and they already planned to do it that way."

Olina allowed herself to be led out of the warm building into the cold of a spring midnight in Minnesota. Stars twinkled in the clear inky sky above. Shivering, she pulled her woolen shawl tighter around her and threw the loose end across her shoulder. She had done a good job of not thinking about Lars, but for a moment, she couldn't stop thinking how good it would feel to have his arms around her to help keep out the cold. She imagined glancing up into his gray eyes, but instead the eyes she saw in her mind were glittering, icy blue.

❧

Anna smiled up at Gustaf. "I missed you while you were on your trip to New York. I've been surprised that you haven't come over since you returned. You've been back three weeks, haven't you?"

Gustaf's nod was accompanied by a grunt of assent.

"I suppose you've been busy catching up with the things that didn't get done while you were gone."

"That's right." Gustaf steered her toward the door. "I'm glad you wore this cape. It'll be warm on the ride home." Gustaf was trying to change the subject, but this was not a good subject to change to.

"Well, you could keep me warm," Anna purred in a voice

unlike her usual clear one.

It was a good thing Gustaf was walking behind her. She couldn't see him gritting his teeth. How was he going to do this without hurting her too much? Even though the cold air caressed them as they walked to the buggy, Gustaf was beginning to sweat. This night was going to end in disaster. It wouldn't end well for him and not for Anna, either.

After helping Anna into the buggy, Gustaf walked around in front of the horses, giving them an encouraging pat as he passed. When he climbed up on the seat, he noticed that Anna was sitting closer to the middle than the side. Gustaf didn't want to sit so close to her.

He didn't want her upset the whole way home. It would take about half an hour to get to the Jenson farm. He would wait until they were within sight of the farmhouse to talk to her.

As they drove along, Anna kept up a steady stream of chatter. Gustaf wasn't sure what she was talking about because he was trying to think how to say what he needed to say with the least amount of hurt. He hoped his occasional comments of *yes, right,* and *interesting* were appropriate and at the right time.

When they were still about a mile from the Jenson farmhouse, Anna broke through his thoughts. "All right, Gustaf." Her voice was louder and harsher than it had been on the rest of the trip. "Are you going to tell me what's bothering you?"

Gustaf pulled the team off the road and parked under a tree. He tied the reins to the front of the buggy and sat there a minute. Then he turned to look at Anna in the dark shadows. Her luminous eyes sparkled through the darkness. "What makes you think something's the matter?" It was a stupid question. They had spent enough time together for her to read his moods.

"I've been carrying on a one-sided conversation all the way home. You haven't heard a single word I've said." Anna sat with her arms crossed defiantly across her chest.

Gustaf wanted to deny her allegation, but then thought better of it. "You're right. My thoughts have been engaged otherwise."

"And who has engaged your thoughts?"

Gustaf was amazed that her question had cut straight to the root of the problem, but he didn't want to tell her that right now.

Sensing his hesitation, Anna continued, "Are you going to tell me what's going on?"

"Anna." Gustaf tried to take her hand in his, but she pulled stiffly to the far end of the buggy seat. He was afraid if he reached for her again, she might tumble off into the dirt. He didn't want that.

"I've been thinking about our relationship." Gustaf stopped and cleared his throat, trying to dislodge the large lump that had taken up residence there.

"And?" Anna wasn't going to make this any easier.

"And. . ." Gustaf tried again. "And I think. . .maybe. . .we shouldn't spend so much time together."

"Is there someone else?" Anna's bitter question surprised Gustaf.

"What kind of man do you think I am?" he asked in anger.

"I don't know what kind of man you are." Anna shivered, but she pulled even farther away from him, if that was possible. "I thought—" Anna stopped to swallow a sob. "I thought we had something. You've been calling on me for some time now."

An owl hooted in a nearby tree, and the wind picked up, swishing the branches above their heads.

"Well. . .I have been." That lump had grown to be a boulder. "Calling on you, I mean." Why did this have to be so hard to say? "I'm not sure we're supposed to be together for life."

Even in the dark, he could see Anna glare at him. "What is that supposed to mean?" Her tone was harder and more brittle.

"I thought you were going to ask me to marry you tonight." Anna ended on a sob, and Gustaf could see the tears glistening on her cheeks, making trails that she didn't wipe off.

It felt as if there were a dagger in his heart. He reached out to her, but hesitated when he saw her expression. Gustaf pulled his big white handkerchief from his back pocket and handed it to her, knowing she wouldn't want him touching her right now. As she mopped her tears away, they were replaced by others.

"I know that's what you thought, and that makes this even harder." Gustaf tried to sound gentle, but he didn't. The words sounded harsh to his own ears. "You're important to me, but I know I don't love you the way you should be loved by your future husband. You deserve better than that. Can't we remain friends?"

"And are we friends right now?" Anna's question was forced from between stiff lips. "Is friendship what we have had all this time? Nothing more?"

Gustaf bowed his head and covered his face with both hands. Could the evening get any worse? "I'm so sorry. I didn't want to hurt you." He wasn't even sure Anna heard his muffled words, so he looked up, dropping his hands into his lap.

"Would you please take me home now?"

Gustaf untied the reins and clucked to the waiting horses. Ominous silence accompanied them the last mile to the farmhouse, covering them in an oppressive blanket. When the buggy stopped, Anna didn't wait for Gustaf to help her down. Instead, she scrambled over the wheel, almost falling in her haste.

"Wait, Anna. I'll help you." He tried to follow her.

"Don't bother," she yelled back over her shoulder and ran into the house.

Gustaf hoped some day she would speak to him again.

eight

After the party, Olina settled into life on the Minnesota farm. She gladly helped with her share of the chores. It was good for Gerda and Olina to be together again. It was as if they had never been separated. Gerda helped Olina become a part of the community, and Olina caught Gerda up on what had happened in the old country after the Nilssons left.

Before long, the two girls spent most of their evenings doing needlework as they talked. Gerda took an interest in all the fashionable clothes Olina had brought with her from Europe.

"Stand still, Olina." Gerda walked around her friend, looking at the darts and flounces on the dark green traveling suit Olina was modeling. "I want to see how she made this."

"I could take it off." Olina unbuttoned the suit. "That way we could look at the seams from the inside. The jacket is lined, but the waist and skirt aren't." When the coat was completely removed, it revealed a soft creamy cotton waist with a lace-edged, ruffled jabot gracefully draping around Olina's neck.

Just then, the back door burst open and Gustaf entered, followed by his brother August. Gerda and Olina watched them from the parlor.

"I tell you, Gustaf." August raised his voice. "You'll never get him to sell it."

"What need does he have for a plow horse?" Gustaf sounded disgusted. "That horse will stay in his barn and pasture and never do another day's work." He threw his cap on the table, stomped over to the sink, and started washing his hands.

"I could use another plow horse."

August glanced through the door to the parlor and saw the two girls. "Gerda, how are you?" He rushed to his sister, picked her up and twirled her around, then set her on her feet. "It's been a long time since I saw you."

Gustaf followed him, drying his hands as he went. "You saw her on Sunday. It's only Thursday. That's not a long time."

He stopped short when he saw Olina. She was standing between him and the window. The sun coming through the pane gave her a gilt edge, turning the soft hairs that had escaped her chignon into a golden halo. The creamy-colored blouse and dark green skirt looked like something from one of the *Godey's Lady's Books* Gerda often received. Olina took his breath away.

It had been like this ever since he talked to Anna. He had felt a freedom from his ties to her, releasing all the pent-up feelings for Olina he had been fighting before.

Sometimes the pain he glimpsed deep in her eyes, when she didn't know anyone was looking, cut him to the quick. He knew Lars had hurt her, but Gustaf felt that there was even more hurt he didn't know about. What could it be?

Besides, Olina didn't ever participate in worship when they were in church. The Sandstrom family and the Nilsson family had been part of the same church in Sweden. Both families fully participated in everything together. During the services now, Olina looked as if she had been turned to stone. If only he could reach across the barriers and ease the pain in her. But how could he do that? He prayed for her every day. He tried to reach out to her in subtle ways.

"Are you men coming in for the evening?" Gerda turned from August to Gustaf.

"We thought we'd sit and talk awhile before August returns to town." Gustaf lowered himself onto the horsehair sofa. "Do you girls want to visit with us?"

Olina looked at Gerda. "If we want to discover how the seamstress made this suit, maybe we should go up to my room." She swept out of the parlor and up the stairs without waiting for an answer.

ھ

When the two young women reached the bedroom, Olina stepped out of the skirt. She handed the garment to Gerda before also shedding her waist and putting on her dressing gown.

"Look at all the tucks and ruffles she made on this waist." She knew she was hiding from Gustaf, but she didn't like the way he unsettled her. The feelings aroused by being near him were at war with the decision she made not to trust a man again. Turning from her musings, she looked into the questioning face of Gerda. "I wonder how long it took her to finish the waist of the suit."

This question didn't deter Gerda. "Olina, what's the matter?"

Olina looked away and picked up the garment she had been talking about.

"Oh, don't worry." Gerda stood looking into Olina's troubled eyes. "I don't think anyone else has noticed. But I've known you too long not to see that something more is wrong."

Olina crumpled onto the side of the bed. Gerda sat beside Olina and pulled her into her arms. How could she comfort her? She didn't even know exactly what was wrong.

"You can tell me what it is. I'll keep your secret." The whispered words went to Olina's heart. "Sometimes it helps to have someone to talk to. Someone who knows everything. You know that nothing you could tell me would ever change the way I feel about you. We're too good of friends for that, ja?"

Olina nodded as she raised her head from her friend's shoulder. "I have been carrying this a long time, and it has become an unbearable burden. . . . But I don't know where to begin."

"Since I know about Lars"—Gerda reached up to brush back the hair that had fallen across Olina's forehead—"why not tell me what else is bothering you?"

Olina stood and walked across the room. She stood at the window and pulled back the filmy curtains. Dusk was falling on the farm, wrapping all the buildings and trees in shadows. She stared into the shifting darkness.

"It's hard to tell you that my own father doesn't love me."

Gerda's quickly indrawn breath preceded her question. "How can you say that? Your family has always been close."

"I thought so." Olina looked toward the sky to see the first twinklings of starlight. "But you know that father was always stern. He's a very controlling man."

Gerda stood and crossed the room to stand beside her. "That doesn't mean he doesn't love you."

Olina turned and gazed into her friend's face. "He disowned me when I chose to come to America and marry Lars."

Gerda stood speechless. Olina could see that she was trying to digest what she had just heard. "Disowned you? What do you mean?"

"He told me that I was no longer a part of the family. . .that I was to have no contact with anyone in my family." She started pacing back and forth across the bedroom, before returning to stand beside the window.

"What about your mother and your brothers?" Gerda demanded.

"They could say nothing. Father was in a high temper. I think he thought I would change my mind, but I couldn't. Lars and I were so in love." Olina finished on a sob, dropping to the floor. She crossed her arms on the windowsill and placed her chin on her hands. "At least I *was* in love with him," she wailed.

Gerda dropped beside Olina and once again held her in her arms. "Your father will change his mind."

Olina looked up. "That's what Tant Olga said. She said he'd change his mind when we had his grandchildren. But now that will never happen." Olina felt completely drained. "How could God have allowed all this?"

The question hung in the air between the two young women. A question without an answer.

Gerda got up and started picking up the clothing they had dropped at various places around the room. "Olina, didn't you write your father a letter right after you arrived?"

Olina nodded. "I told him what happened, and I asked him to send me the money to come home. I told him I would work and pay back every cent as soon as I could."

"Well, see. Everything will be all right. He'll send you the money." Gerda folded the skirt and laid it across the end of the bed.

Olina stood and picked up the crumpled waist from where the two girls had sat on it. Smoothing out the wrinkles the best she could, she put it beside the skirt. "But what if he doesn't? What will I do then?" She turned a forlorn face toward her friend.

Gerda took Olina by the shoulders. "He will. He has to." She let go and picked up the jacket. "But if he doesn't, you'll stay right here."

"I can't stay here. I would be a burden to your family."

"A burden? I don't think so." Gerda turned the jacket wrong side out. "You've been doing your part. Besides that, maybe we could move to town together and become seamstresses. We're both good at making quality clothing. The only ready-made clothing at the mercantile has to be ordered from other places, and they never fit right. We could probably make a good living as seamstresses. The only way Father will let me move to town is if I have someone to live with. It would work out well for both of us." Gerda smiled at Olina. "Besides, it won't come to that. You'll be going home before you know it. So let's do all we can to learn how she made your lovely clothes. *Jaha?*"

nine

When Olina came, the Nilsson family had started speaking Swedish most of the time around Olina so she would not feel left out. Olina asked Gerda to help her learn English, and Gerda was good about helping her. After the second week, she asked the whole family to speak mostly English, so she could learn it. Even if she went back to Sweden, she would be glad she knew the language. Olina was surprised how quickly she picked it up. It wasn't easy, but when she heard it all the time, it was easier to learn. Now that she had been there nearly two months, only a few Swedish words crept into their conversations.

Gerda and Olina took each of the garments Olina had brought as part of her trousseau and studied it inside and out. They drew diagrams of how each piece was shaped and how the pieces fit together. Then they made new summer dresses from some fabric they had at the farm.

"Moder," Gerda called out as the two girls came down the stairs carrying one of the new dresses. "Come see what we have for you." Both girls were excited.

Mrs. Nilsson wiped her hands on her big white apron as she came from the kitchen into the hallway. "Now what could you possibly have for me? No one has been to town today."

"We wanted to surprise you." Olina held the dress up by the shoulders. It fell to the floor in a graceful sweep. "Here, try it on."

Mrs. Nilsson was surprised, but pleased. "All this time I thought you girls were making something pretty for yourselves."

"We did." Gerda twirled to show off her new dress. "This is

mine." Balloon sleeves, gathered at the shoulder and tightly cuffed at her wrists, had five rows of tucks running the entire length. Intricate white lace set off the powder blue material with a dainty flower pattern. The dress was full at the bust, but had the new wasp waist that was accented by the full skirt. Yards of material gathered at the waist and swept to dust the floor with a lace trimmed ruffle flounce.

"See, Mrs. Nilsson, we made you one like hers." Olina held it out to her. "Only in an old rose floral print."

"I'm too old to wear such frippery." Mrs. Nilsson couldn't keep a smile from flitting across her face as she reached for the dress and held it up in front of her.

"You are not." Gerda hugged her mother. "It'll look good on you."

The girls went into the parlor to wait for Mrs. Nilsson to return. Someone had brought in the mail, and it contained a new *Godey's*. The two girls pored over the pages while they waited.

"Mrs. Johnson gave me a stack of these magazines that she had collected over the years. I had a good time looking through them. I don't think the book is as good since Sarah Hale sold it." Gerda was looking at some of the pictures. "I'm not sure how long I will continue to take it."

"It does help you keep up with fashion, doesn't it?"

"Anna has been taking another magazine. It's called *Ladies Home Journal*. I'm sure she would let us borrow one to compare them."

Just then Mrs. Nilsson came in wearing the new dress. "This is wonderful." She smoothed the fabric over her hips. "You put more lace on mine than you did yours." Lace lined the tucks on her sleeve and outlined the waspish waist. The delicate rose color of the dress brought out the natural color in her cheeks, making her look younger. "I'm sure you had a hand in this."

She smiled at Olina.

"Gerda helped. And she picked out the fabric for you. It does look good." Olina had a feeling of accomplishment when she looked at the beautiful picture made by the woman standing before her.

Mrs. Nilsson continued to finger the delicate lace. "When the other women see these dresses and how well they fit, you'll probably have some asking you to make them a dress."

That sounded good to Olina. If her father refused to send her the money to come home, maybe she and Gerda could work together.

"What have we here?" Mr. Nilsson's voice boomed, preceding him from the hallway into the parlor. "Who is this vision of loveliness?" He picked his wife up from behind and twirled her around before setting her feet back on the floor.

"Bennel, behave yourself." Mrs. Nilsson blushed and patted a hair back in place.

"Where did my Ingrid get this pretty dress? I haven't seen it before, have I?" His expression told the girls how much he liked the garment.

"No. The girls made it for me as a surprise."

Mr. Nilsson looked astonished. "I thought you had to try it on several times to check the fit."

"I did, too. But they made it in secret, and it fits so well." She turned around so he could see the dress from every angle.

"You girls are good." Pride tinged his voice. "Very good."

"Mother," Gerda interrupted, "we used the last of the light-weight fabric we have here. Maybe Olina and I need to go to town and pick out some more."

"I could take you," Gustaf said from the hallway.

His voice startled Olina. When had he come in? She hadn't heard the door open. She had been too wrapped up in what was going on.

"I'm going to town tomorrow." Gustaf was drying his hands on a towel from the kitchen, so he had been in the house long enough to wash his hands. "You girls can ride along. How about it?"

"Sure," Gerda answered before Olina could decline.

Olina knew she should refuse. She had little money. She wanted to keep what little she had in case her father refused to send her the money to go home.

All eyes had turned to her, and she needed to give an answer. It might not hurt to ride along with them. She might have to tell Gerda why she was not spending her money, but she didn't want the rest of the family to know that Fader had rejected her when she left Sweden. That was one secret she was in no hurry to share.

After supper, the girls were upstairs in Olina's room looking at more of the drawings they had made. Gerda picked out four of them.

"I want to get fabric to make these four for me." She pointed out two more of them. "Mother would look good in these. What kind of fabric are you going to buy?"

Olina looked at the floor for a minute. She traced the pattern in the carpet with the toe of her black high-top shoe. "I won't be buying any."

"Why not?"

"I don't want to spend the money I have left. I might need it."

"Don't worry about that. We'll get you some fabric with our order."

"I couldn't take it." Olina looked up at her friend. "Besides, I have all these new clothes I brought with me."

⋙

Soon after breakfast, Gustaf pulled the wagon to the front of the house. The day was fresh and new as the girls stepped out into the brisk morning air. The sun had come up, and the rooster was still occasionally crowing as he pranced across the yard.

When they reached the wagon, Olina was trying to figure out how she could get up without Gustaf touching her. Then he placed his hands on her waist and swung her effortlessly across the wagon wheel. In the blink of an eye, she was sitting on the bench seat beside Gerda.

Gustaf walked around the front of the wagon. He stopped by each horse and gave it a bite of something he had in his pocket. Olina watched him, all the while still feeling where the heat of his hands had touched her. Her skin burned, and her stomach was in turmoil. This was going to be a long day.

"You haven't been to town, except to go to church, have you, Olina?" Gustaf's voice broke through her thoughts.

"No, not since the day I arrived," she whispered.

"How long have you been here?" Gustaf picked up the reins and clicked his tongue to start the horses.

Was the man going to ask her questions all the way to town? "It's been about two months, hasn't it?" she said.

Gerda looked at Olina and must have noticed how uncomfortable she was, because she changed the subject. "Gustaf, we haven't seen Anna since the night of the party. And you have not gone over to the Jensons', have you?"

Gustaf's face seemed to close up. "No," he grunted.

"I'm not trying to make you mad." Gerda looked frustrated. "I was just wondering."

Gustaf heaved a gigantic sigh. "Well, wonder no longer, Little Sister. I have not said anything about it, but Anna and I are not seeing each other any more."

Why did that unsettle Olina? It shouldn't make any difference to her, but a small weight lifted from her heart.

When they reached Litchfield, Gustaf took the young women to the mercantile. He needed to get some work done at the blacksmith's, and he was going by the bank. He promised to return for them in time for the three of them to go to the restaurant at the hotel for lunch.

Gerda pulled Olina along with her as she rushed to see if there were any new bolts of fabric on the shelves. Looking past Gerda, Olina spied several bolts of colorful silk on the shelf beside the cotton bolts.

"Oh, look, Gerda." She pointed to a color that was neither pink nor lavender. "Isn't it lovely?"

Gerda reached for the bolt just as Mrs. Braxton came to help them. "Is this new?"

"We have never had silk this color before. They call it mauve. I think the name is French. Would you like me to cut you some?" Mrs. Braxton reached for the scissors under the counter. "We have refinished this counter so it won't damage the silk."

Olina smoothed her hand across the wooden counter. "It feels nice. It shouldn't snag anything."

Gerda put her finger on her cheek and thought a minute. "I want ten yards of the silk."

"What are you going to make with it?" Olina fingered the fabric, enjoying the smoothness.

"I want to copy one of the dresses you brought with you, and I think I'll make a matching bonnet."

Mrs. Braxton looked at the new dress Gerda was wearing. "Where did you get the pattern for that dress you have on? I like the sleeves. I might want a similar dress myself."

Gerda waved toward her friend. "Olina brought a lot of new clothes with her. We've been studying them. This is the first one we duplicated. Hers was made from a soft, lightweight wool. But it made up really well in this cotton."

"Do you think you could make one to fit me?" Mrs. Braxton turned around so the girls could study her figure. "You could take measurements today."

Gerda looked at Olina with a question in her expression. Olina nodded slightly. It would give her something to do until she heard from Fader.

"I think we could manage that." Gerda turned toward the shop owner's wife. "What fabric do you want us to use?"

Mrs. Braxton reached up and removed a bolt of emerald green silk. "I want it out of this. If you make it for me, I'll give each of you enough fabric to make yourself a dress. . . . Or I could pay you instead."

"I would love to have this sea green silk." Olina held it against herself. "Would I look good in it?"

Gerda nodded. "And I want this. . .what did you call it?"

"Mauve."

"Yes, I'll take the mauve. We each want ten yards."

Mrs. Braxton began cutting the fabric as Gerda and Olina chose thread, buttons, and lace to trim the dresses. Mrs. Braxton added an extra packet of needles to the order before she wrapped it. Then she took the young women upstairs to her living quarters. They spent an hour visiting with Mrs. Braxton while they measured her for her dress and shared a cup of tea with her. They returned downstairs to buy several pieces of calico and gingham to take home. They had finished getting all the notions they needed when Gustaf came for them.

"Are you ready for lunch?"

When Olina heard his voice, she looked up. For a moment she felt drawn to him. What was she thinking? She didn't even trust him. She couldn't risk getting hurt again. All of her pain was still too new. She had tried to deal with it the best she knew how, but she would never risk being hurt like that again.

The three went across the street and entered the dining room of the Excelsior Hotel. It wasn't as luxurious as the hotel where they had stayed in New York City, but it was nice. During the meal, several people Olina met at the party came by the table to visit with them. Lunch passed rather pleasantly.

Just after they finished dessert, Gustaf reached into his pocket for his money. When he did, something crinkled. "I forgot. I picked this up at the post office when I went in to mail some letters." He handed a letter with a Swedish postmark to Olina. "It looks as though you have a letter from home. I know you'll be glad."

Olina didn't want to be impolite, but she couldn't help it. While Gustaf paid the waitress, she tore into the envelope. The thickness of the envelope felt as if the letter would be long and newsy. Instead, the letter she had written home dropped onto the table, unopened. Accompanying it was a short terse note.

> *The person whose return address is on this envelope is considered dead. The Sandstrom family does not want to receive any more mail from that person.*

Olina sat and stared at her father's signature on the bottom of the note.

ða

Gustaf had turned to say something to Gerda when he heard Olina gasp. As he whipped back around, he saw that every bit of color had drained from her face. Her eyes were glazed with unshed tears. Gustaf wanted to shield her from other people, so he got up, gathered the dropped papers from the table, and helped her from the chair. Placing himself between her and the other people in the room, he ushered Olina out the door and through the lobby to the waiting wagon. Gerda followed right behind them.

This time, Gustaf picked Olina up first and put her on the middle of the wagon seat. Gerda could sit on the outside to shield her from curious onlookers. As soon as he was in the wagon, he started the horses toward home. He didn't stop until they pulled up in front of the house.

No one had said anything on the way home. Olina sat quiet and still. When he helped her down from the wagon, she rushed into the house.

"Go to her, Little Sister. She needs someone." Gustaf drove the wagon to the barn, praying for Olina all the way.

ten

He really means it. Olina paced her room, tears streaming down her face. *How can I go on like this?*

Olina wished she could still depend on God. Knowing God was with her had given her comfort when she was younger. She needed comfort now as never before. Gerda had tried to help her, but what could anyone do? Olina dropped in a heap beside her bed, leaning her head on the Flower Garden quilt that draped to the floor. Her shoulders slumped against the side of the bed.

Thinking hurt so much, so Olina tried to clear the horrid thoughts from her mind. However, memories flitted in and out of her head. As she rejected one, another attacked her from the other side. Fader's harsh words the last time she had seen him rang through her consciousness undergirded by the written words on the letter she clutched in a crumpled ball, unable to let go of it. Olina had no hope.

Child, please let me help you. Olina had heard that voice before, but today she turned a deaf ear to it. *I know the plans I have for you.* Olina put her hands on her ears as if to shut out an audible voice and moaned loud enough to drown it out.

Olina stayed in her room for two days, not letting anyone come in except Gerda when she brought food and fresh water. Gerda would return later in the day to pick up the dishes, often containing most of the food, uneaten. But Olina did eat enough to keep from starving. If Gerda hugged Olina, she let her, but when Gerda tried to talk, Olina wouldn't listen. She would busy herself rearranging her silver-handled hairbrush

77

and mirror on the dresser or opening a drawer and moving things around, but she never touched the wad of paper she had finally dropped beside her bed.

The third day, Olina came downstairs after the family had eaten breakfast. When she arrived in the kitchen, Mrs. Nilsson looked up expectantly.

"I don't want to talk about it right now." Olina tried to keep her hostess from asking any questions. "If it's all right, I'll tell the whole family after dinner. That way, I only have to say it once."

Mrs. Nilsson nodded and turned back toward the cabinet. "We have some bacon and biscuits left from breakfast. Are you hungry? I could fix you some eggs." She picked up the cast-iron skillet and placed it on the stove.

"No, thank you." Olina went to the cupboard and got out a plate and glass. "I don't want any eggs, but the biscuits and bacon sound good." She helped herself.

"Would you like some butter and jelly on your biscuits?" Mrs. Nilsson placed a jar of jelly on the table beside the dish of butter.

"That sounds good." Olina pulled out a drawer and picked up a knife and spoon.

"Well, sit down and enjoy your breakfast." Mrs. Nilsson reached for the glass Olina had left on the cabinet. "I'll go to the springhouse and get you some milk."

Olina turned. "Oh, I can get the milk."

"Let me wait on you this one time." Mrs. Nilsson patted Olina on the shoulder. "You haven't let me do much for you since you came here." She turned and started out the back door, but she turned back. "Olina, I want you to know that we've all been praying for you. We were worried, but Gustaf convinced us to let you take your time. He told us that you would talk to us soon." Then she walked into the bright summer sunshine.

Olina sank into a chair by the table. Maybe this wouldn't be so bad. She had been able to function and even carry on a conversation without bursting into tears. If she could get through the day and then the evening, she might make it. Olina hadn't realized how hungry she was. She had eaten two biscuits and two slices of bacon by the time Mrs. Nilsson returned.

"Would you like to finish these other two biscuits and the rest of the bacon?" Mrs. Nilsson picked up the uncovered plate and placed it on the table in front of Olina. "Then I could go ahead and wash up all the dishes."

After breakfast, Olina helped Mrs. Nilsson clean the kitchen before she went out to gather the eggs. Performing regular chores brought the illusion of normalcy to Olina. Egg production had picked up. Although the chickens had a nice house with wooden nests filled with straw, a few of the hens laid their eggs in strange places. When Olina had filled the egg basket from the nests in the henhouse, she searched the weeds that grew along the fence between that building and the barn. There she found three more eggs. Olina went into the barn and looked in the scattered hay at the base of the mound that filled one end of the barn. Four more eggs were added to her basket before she returned to the kitchen.

"Those hens." Olina set the basket on the cabinet. "Why don't they use the nests you've provided for them?"

"I've wondered that myself." Gerda came into the kitchen and put the empty laundry basket on the table.

Olina turned to look at her friend. "At least the ones that lay their eggs somewhere else always lay them in the same places."

Gerda's gaze held Olina's for a minute or two before she turned away. "Ja, that's a good thing. It would take a long time to gather the eggs if we had to search everywhere for them."

Olina was glad that she had seen understanding in Gerda's

expression before she turned away. Having a friend who loved her no matter what could get her through the rest of the day.

&

Dinner was delicious that night. Mrs. Nilsson had baked two large hens. She served them on a platter surrounded by potatoes and carrots. That afternoon, she had also baked fresh bread and an apple pie. It was a feast worthy of a special occasion. Olina tried to eat the wonderful food, but after a few bites, she pushed it around her plate instead of putting it in her mouth. When she thought about the evening ahead, her stomach started jumping and her throat tightened, making it hard to swallow her food.

Mrs. Nilsson looked around the table. "Olina would like to talk to us in the parlor when you're all finished eating."

Gustaf looked up and stared at Olina. Surely he would look away soon. However, he didn't. And Olina couldn't look away, either. Everything in the room faded from her consciousness. It was as if there were only two people in the room, Gustaf and herself. The moment stretched into what seemed like an eternity, and Olina felt more confused than ever. If anyone else noticed, they didn't comment on it.

"We'll help you clean up, Moder." Gustaf got up from his chair and picked up some empty dishes from the table.

"You don't have to do that." Mrs. Nilsson reached for them.

"Yes, we do." Gustaf continued toward the sink with his hands full. "That way we'll all get to the parlor at the same time."

Even Mr. Nilsson helped. Gustaf and Gerda started talking about what they had done during the day. Soon the dishes were washed and put away. Mrs. Nilsson removed her big white apron and hung it on a hook beside the back door.

By the time Olina reached the parlor, the only place to sit was beside Gerda on the sofa. When she was seated, everyone turned toward Olina. The time had come for her to share. She closed her eyes and took a deep breath. Before she opened them again, Gerda reached over, took her hand, and squeezed it.

❧

Gustaf's heart ached as he watched Olina prepare to talk to them. When he had looked at her during dinner, he could see the wall she had erected around her heart. It was painted with painful strokes trying to hide what was inside, but he could see more hurt than he ever wanted to feel himself. He wondered how she could take it. She didn't look that strong, but she must be.

When Gustaf had gone into the kitchen for dinner, she had been standing beside her chair. He thought she looked fragile when he had met her on the dock, but that woman would look strong beside the woman standing by the table. She had to have inner strength to stand there, as if nothing were wrong. But something was wrong, terribly wrong. *Gud, what can I do to help her. Please tell me.*

He wished he could sit beside her, where Gerda was. He wanted to be the one to comfort her and take away her pain. This feeling was new and stronger than anything he had ever felt for a woman. Was this love? If it was, what could he do about it if she wouldn't let him come near her?

Just love her, My son. She needs so much love.

When Olina opened her eyes, Gustaf tried to communicate that love to her through his expression. He knew he would have to go slowly and let God heal Olina's hurts before he could ever say anything to her about his feelings. That thought caused his heart to beat a little faster. Gustaf felt hope for a day when Olina might be his wife.

❧

Olina glanced at Gustaf. He was looking right at her. His expression was trying to tell her something, but she felt uncomfortable, so she quickly looked away. What was he trying to communicate to her?

Olina took a deep breath again. Still holding Gerda's hand, she looked at Mr. Nilsson and then Mrs. Nilsson before fixing her gaze on the pattern in the carpet. As she began to talk, she studied the design.

"I'm sorry I have not been sociable these last two days."

Gerda didn't let her continue. "Olina, it's all right."

"Yes," Mrs. Nilsson added. "You have no need to apologize."

Olina nodded. "Thank you." She looked into Mrs. Nilsson's sweet face. "I seem to have a serious problem." For a moment she couldn't go on. A large lump formed in her throat, and she couldn't get any words around it.

Gustaf jumped up from the chair where he was sitting and went to the kitchen. He could be heard rummaging around before he returned with a glass of water. When he reached toward Olina, she gladly took the proffered liquid refreshment.

After a few sips of the cool well water, she was able to continue. "My father didn't want me to come to America. He told me that if I did, he would disown me. I didn't think he really meant it. . .until I received the reply to my letter."

Olina's hands started shaking, so she set the glass on the table beside the sofa. "He didn't even open my letter. Instead, he wrote that the person who mailed it was considered dead by the family. He doesn't want me to write again."

A sob was working its way up Olina's throat, but by sheer will, she swallowed it. She wouldn't cry in front of everyone.

"I have no home."

"You certainly do," Mr. Nilsson thundered. "Your home is right here." He jumped out of his chair as if catapulted and stomped toward the hall. He leaned one hand on the door frame, looking as if he needed the support. With his head down, he paused before he turned around and continued. "We are your family now." He looked as if he wanted to say something more, but instead, he turned and walked through the kitchen. Before he went out the back door, Olina saw him grab his hat from the hook and slam it on his head.

Mrs. Nilsson spoke softly. "You'll have to forgive him, Olina. When he's disturbed, he tends to get too loud."

Olina nodded. "That's all right."

"He really does love you." Mrs. Nilsson got up from the rocking chair and walked over to Olina. "I know you are concerned about not having any money. You're doing your share around here, so you will be treated like the others."

Olina started to say something, but Gerda interrupted. "Besides, we've started making dresses. Perhaps we'll soon make enough money to live on."

Gustaf had been sitting listening to everyone else. When he heard what Gerda said, he stood up and made a noise that sounded like a snort. Olina looked up at him, and he said, "Neither one of you needs to make enough money to live on. We'll take care of you." Then he followed his father out the back door.

What was it about men that they felt they had to take care of women? The two men who should have taken care of Olina hadn't. She never wanted to have to depend on a man again.

eleven

Gerda and Olina were hanging clothes on the line when they noticed a horse-drawn surrey turn from the country road and start up the long drive to the house. With her right hand, Gerda shaded her eyes from the bright sunlight and gazed at the approaching vehicle.

Olina removed a wooden peg-shaped clothespin from her mouth and secured a sheet to the rope line. "Is that someone you know?"

"The surrey belongs to the Braxtons." Gerda picked up another pillowcase from the laundry basket. "It looks as if Mrs. Braxton is driving, and she has another woman with her. Did Moder say anything this morning at breakfast about expecting company?"

"I didn't hear her." Olina stopped and, while Gerda hung the final piece of laundry on the line, watched the two women as they moved closer and closer to the house.

Gerda picked up the empty laundry basket. "I thought maybe I wasn't paying attention. Come on. We don't often get unexpected company."

The young women went in through the back door before the knock sounded on the front. Mrs. Nilsson looked up from the stove, where she was stirring a pot of stew.

"Now who can that be?" She patted a stray lock of hair into place and started untying her apron strings. "Did you see any-one drive up?"

"Mrs. Braxton and another woman," Olina answered while Gerda hung the laundry basket on a hook beside the back door.

Gerda turned to her mother. "I think it might be her sister-in-law. The one who is married to Mr. Braxton's brother."

Mrs. Nilsson brushed her hands down her skirt to smooth it. "The one from Denver?" When Gerda frowned and glanced at Olina, she stopped talking.

"I forgot they were coming to town for a visit." Mrs. Nilsson started toward the front door.

"Denver?" Olina looked at Gerda. "Is he the man who owns the store where Lars went to work when he moved to Denver?"

Gerda slowly nodded, not taking her gaze from her friend's face.

Olina took a deep breath. "I think I'll go to my room." She hurried through the hall and up the stairs before Mrs. Nilsson had invited her guests into the house.

❧

"Do come in." Mrs. Nilsson opened the door wide and gestured toward the parlor.

The two women preceded her into the room. After sitting on the sofa, they started removing their gloves.

Mrs. Nilsson sat in her favorite rocker. "It's always a nice surprise to have guests come to your door. Besides, I want to know how Lars is doing."

Mrs. Braxton glanced at her sister-in-law, who said, "He was fine when we left Denver."

"Actually. . ." Mrs. Braxton looked around. "We were hoping to talk to Gerda and Olina."

Gerda was starting up the stairs to check on Olina when she heard her own name spoken. She came back down the steps and entered the parlor.

"Gerda is right here." Mrs. Nilsson looked at her. "Do you know where Olina is?"

"She went upstairs." Gerda sat in the straight chair where she could see both the staircase and the other women in the parlor.

"Let me go put some tea to steep while you talk to Gerda." Mrs. Nilsson started toward the kitchen. "Then I'll go see about Olina."

❧

Olina was standing at her favorite place beside the window, watching two birds with their babies in a nest in the tree by the barn, when she heard a soft knock on her door. She had been expecting someone, but she had figured it would be Gerda, not her mother. Gerda always knocked harder. Olina glanced one more time at the industrious birds before she started toward the door. *I wish I could be like you. You don't seem to have a worry in the world.*

Olina took a deep breath before she opened the door and peeked around the edge. "Yes?"

"The ladies would like to see you and Gerda." Mrs. Nilsson's compassionate look went to Olina's heart. "But you don't have to come down. . .if you don't want to."

Olina sighed. "It's okay. I have to face people sooner or later." She fluffed her hair where the kerchief had mashed it while she was hanging up the clothes. "I'm feeling better since I told your family everything last week." She stepped through the door and closed it behind her.

Mrs. Nilsson put her arm around Olina's waist. "I'm proud of you, Olina."

They went down the stairs together. When they entered the parlor, Mrs. Braxton looked up eagerly.

"Olina, there you are." She stood and took Olina's hand in both of hers. "My sister-in-law wanted to meet you two."

Olina looked at the other woman still sitting on the sofa. The woman was smiling at her. Olina wondered how much she might know about what had happened, if she knew that Olina had come to America to marry Lars.

"Olina, this is Sophia." Mrs. Braxton took Olina by the arm and led her farther into the room. "She was wondering how long it would take you and Gerda to make her some dresses."

Olina looked at Gerda. This was what they were hoping for. "How many dresses are we talking about?"

Sophia Braxton rose from where she was sitting. "We're going to be here in Litchfield for a week before we return to Denver. We were in Chicago, but I didn't see any clothes there that could compare with the dress you made Marja." She looked at her sister-in-law. "Without a dressmaker, I can't get clothes that fit as well as her dress does. I would like to have as many dresses as you can make during the week we are here. I understand that you brought several European fashions with you when you came."

Olina wondered if she looked as surprised as Gerda did. How many dresses could they make in a week? They didn't know.

Marja looked from one girl to the other. "I have an idea."

"What?" Olina and Gerda both said at once.

Marja clapped her hands before clasping them under her chin. "You girls could stay in town this week. That way you would be close if you need to do any fitting."

Olina was amazed. She would have never thought of that.

"But where would they stay?" Mrs. Nilsson looked worried.

"They could stay at the hotel." Sophia stood up. "What a wonderful idea. Adolph could rent the room next to ours. I think it's empty."

The idea presented interesting possibilities to Olina. If all they did that week was sew, they might make quite a bit of money.

Marja chuckled. "I'm full of ideas. The price on treadle sewing machines has dropped, so we ordered one for the store. It came last week. Maybe you girls could use it. I've heard that you can sew much faster that way."

Olina looked at Gerda. Sew with a machine? She had never used one. All the dresses she had made were by hand. "I wouldn't know how to use it."

"It has a manual." Marja patted Olina's arm. "We could learn how to use it together. That would help Mr. Braxton and me sell more of the machines, if we know how well they work."

It would be a change from staying on the farm. Maybe it was not a bad idea. Olina turned toward Mrs. Nilsson.

"Do you think Mr. Nilsson would mind?"

"We could ask him."

❧

When the men came in for dinner, Gerda and Olina had a hard time keeping their questions to themselves. They wanted to blurt out what Mrs. Braxton had said, but they knew they needed to wait. It seemed as if the men took an eternity washing up, but finally, they were all seated around the table. After the blessing, Mrs. Nilsson started passing food around the table.

"We had some visitors today." She smiled at the girls as she made the casual comment. "Marja Braxton and her sister-in-law Sophia came by."

Mr. Nilsson put a large scoop of gravy on his mashed potatoes, then passed the gravy boat along to Gustaf. "What did Mrs. Braxton have to say? Did she have any news of Lars?" After realizing what he had said, Mr. Nilsson blushed and looked at Olina.

Mrs. Nilsson took a bite of her baked chicken. She chewed and swallowed it before answering. "She said he was fine when she left Denver. She didn't come to see me. She wanted to talk to the girls."

Mr. Nilsson looked first at Gerda, then Olina. "Why would she want to talk to our lovely girls?"

Gerda giggled. "She wants us to sew for her sister-in-law."

"You remember when the girls made the dress for Marja?" Mrs. Nilsson put her hand on her husband's arm. "They did such a good job that she recommended them to Sophia."

Mr. Nilsson nodded. "Good work speaks for itself."

"They want the girls to spend the week in town, so they can sew all week for Sophia."

The girls held their breath while they waited for Mr. Nilsson to answer. However, they knew he couldn't be rushed.

Mr. Nilsson thought for a moment. "That might not be a bad idea. Where would they stay? Do the Braxtons have enough room for all the extra people?"

"Well." Mrs. Nilsson took a drink of water. "The Braxtons' living quarters are small, so Adolph and Sophia are staying at the hotel. They want to rent the room next to them for the girls."

Mr. Nilsson put his fork down and rested his forearms on the table. He looked from his wife to his daughter to Olina. "Is that right?"

"Oh, Fader, Mrs. Braxton has a treadle sewing machine in the store." Gerda pleaded with her father. "She wants us to use it so we can get several dresses done this week. Would it be all right if we go? Please?"

Mr. Nilsson looked at his wife. "Do you think it's a good idea? I wouldn't want anything to happen to the girls."

Mrs. Nilsson nodded. "I'm sure Johan and Marja and Adolph and Sophia would protect them."

"Let me think about it a bit." Mr. Nilsson picked up his fork.

"If you decide it's all right, I would be glad to take Gerda and Olina into town in the morning." Gustaf looked at his father. "I need to pick up a plow August is fixing for me. He said it would be ready by tomorrow."

Mr. Nilsson took another bite and laid his fork down while

he chewed his food. He looked at Gerda, then Olina. "I think that is a good idea."

Gerda jumped up from her chair. "That's wonderful." She went to her father and hugged him.

Olina had finished packing her carpetbag when Gerda knocked on her door.

"I can hardly believe Father agreed to let us go. It'll be so much fun."

"It will be a lot of work, too." Olina smiled at her friend's enthusiasm. She walked over to the window for a last look at the birds. "I wonder if the babies will learn to fly by the time we get back from town?"

"What?" Gerda came up beside her.

Olina pointed toward a fork in a high branch. "See that nest? I have been watching the birds with their babies."

"Maybe they will." Gerda picked up Olina's bag. It felt light. "You aren't taking much for a week's stay."

"I don't need much to work all day." Olina laughed.

Gerda stopped at the door and turned around. "We'll do more than just sew all the time. There's always something going on in town."

Olina wasn't interested in what was going on in town. She wanted to see how much money she could make as a dressmaker. Maybe she could soon support herself. But would Mr. Nilsson let her live on her own?

The ride into town was a happy affair. Gustaf and Gerda teased each other and told funny stories. Olina relaxed and enjoyed the comradery. She missed being around her brothers, and this brought back pleasant memories. If only she could keep from thinking about Fader and the pain he had caused her. Because of him, she would never see her brothers again. She couldn't think about that or she would cry. So she shut out those thoughts and chuckled at Gerda and Gustaf.

৯

When Olina first laughed, Gustaf almost fell off the wagon seat. He thought he would never hear that laugh again. Ever since Olina had told them about her family, she had hardly smiled when he was around. He didn't know if she smiled at other times. He turned to look at her.

She was wearing a light green dress and bonnet. Probably one she and Gerda had been working on. He remembered their buying green fabric when they went to town. The color brought out the peachy texture of her skin. A light wind tugged some of her hair free from the confines of the hat, and the sun shining through it made it look like liquid gold floating in the air around her head. She was so beautiful. It almost hurt to look at her. He wanted to take her in his arms and hold her close, but he knew he couldn't do that yet.

"Gustaf." Gerda was looking at him. "You haven't answered my question."

He dragged his gaze from the beautiful image he was enjoying and glanced at his sister. "What did you ask?"

"See," she said to Olina. "He wasn't even listening to me."

Olina laughed. "I guess not."

"Well, what did you want to know?" Gustaf tried to sound gruff.

"How long will you stay in town today?"

Gustaf looked at Olina again. A sinking feeling settled in his stomach. He didn't want to leave her in town. Every day he looked forward to sitting across from her at the dinner table. Often he saw her during the day as she worked around the farm, gathering eggs or hanging up clothes or walking around and enjoying the outdoors. He was always finding excuses to work near her, so they could talk to each other. The longer he was around her, the more he found to admire about her.

"I may be there most of the day." He turned toward the

outskirts of town that were up ahead. "If that's all right with you."

"Of course it is." Gerda hugged his arm. "You can help us get settled. That way, you can assure Father that we are all right."

"Sounds like a good idea." Gustaf smiled. *A very good idea. Maybe I'll have to find several reasons to come to town this week. So I can assure Father that they're all right.* But he didn't fool himself. He wanted to come to town to see Olina as much as possible. *Yes, this week could get interesting.*

twelve

When Gustaf stopped the wagon in front of the mercantile, Marja and Sophia Braxton hurried out the front door. They must have been as eager as Gerda and Olina, since they had been watching for them.

"Mrs. Braxton." Gustaf doffed his cap. "Should I take the girls to the hotel? Their bags are in the wagon."

"What a wonderful idea." Marja clapped her hands. "Sophia and I'll walk over right now."

"I'm sorry I can't offer you a ride." Gustaf gave a rueful smile. "The wagon seat is full. If you want to wait, I can come back for you."

"It's not far, and the walk will do us good." Sophia waved them off.

Gerda's eyes sparkled as she looked around. "I'm so excited. I didn't think Father would let us do this."

Gustaf chuckled. "You're a grown woman, Gerda. Father wants the best for you. He's just careful because sometimes there are rough men in town."

"I know." Gerda put her hands around his powerful arm and looked up into his face. "We'll be careful." She turned to look at her friend. "Right, Olina?"

"Of course." Olina made the mistake of looking at Gustaf. His gaze was fastened on her, and when she looked at him, she was drawn to those blue eyes. Sometimes, they could look so icy, but now they held the warmth of a sunshiny day. That warmth reached all the way to her toes. She couldn't look away, even if she had wanted to. But she didn't want to.

That warmth was melting something deep inside her, as the sunshine melted ice in the fjords back home.

Home? Where was home? Was it in Sweden? Or was it right here in Minnesota with people who accepted her for who she was. People who didn't try to change her. Yes, it was starting to feel like home. With a tremulous smile, Olina finally looked away from Gustaf's mesmerizing eyes. Today was a new day. Minnesota was her new home. Olina was going to make the best of it.

Child, let Me help you.

Olina almost heeded the quiet voice. Almost, but not quite.

≈

When Olina smiled, Gustaf could feel it touch his heart. It felt like the wings of a butterfly as it flitted across the flowers Gerda planted around the front porch. Soft, gentle, but a smile nonetheless. Olina needed to smile more. Maybe this was the start of something in her life. She looked as if she had made a discovery. . .or a resolution. Gustaf didn't know which. But whichever it was, it would have far-reaching consequences in her life. He hoped those consequences would include him. *Please, Gud.*

≈

Adolph Braxton was waiting in the hotel lobby for them. He took them up to the third floor, the top floor. "We wanted to be away from the noise in the street."

He opened the door to a large room that was at the back corner of the hotel. Windows on adjoining walls bathed the interior with sunlight.

Olina walked over to check the view. Since the hotel was taller than the building next door, she could look across the rooftops. The hotel was at the end of Main Street, so the windows at the back overlooked an open field.

Olina turned around. "This is a wonderful room. We'll have

lots of light to work by."

Just then, Marja and Sophia walked in. Marja smiled and clapped her hands. "We thought this would be just right. Sophia and Adolph moved next door so you girls could have this room."

"You didn't have to do that," Gerda exclaimed.

"Nonsense." Sophia put her arm through her husband's. "This room is the largest in the hotel. It'll give you plenty of space to work. Our room is nice, too." She smiled up at her husband. "Right, Dear?"

Adolph nodded. It looked to Olina as if his fair skin blushed a little under his bushy sideburns.

"We'll bring the sewing machine up later today," Marja said.

"Mrs. Braxton." Gustaf walked to the door. "Would you like me to bring it in my wagon? I would be glad to."

With a harrumph, Adolph said he would help Gustaf, and the two men left. Olina looked around. Heavy drapes hung at the windows. Olina walked over and discovered ties hanging high beside the window. She used them to hold the drapes open and allow the maximum of light to enter the room. Gerda went to the large canopy bed that was in one corner of the room. She sat on the side. Olina turned and surveyed the room. Even with the substantial wardrobe on the wall near the door and the table that sat against the other wall without a window, there was lots of space. There were even two straight chairs by the table. This would be a wonderful place to work.

"This room is as large as some people's houses," Gerda said as she walked to one of the two rocking chairs that flanked a small round table.

Sophia sat in one of the rockers. "That's why we wanted you to have this room. You can spread out all over while you are working."

While they were waiting for the men to return, Olina and Gerda showed their drawings of the clothing to the two Mrs. Braxtons. Sophia exclaimed over most of them.

"How am I ever going to choose which dresses for you to make for me?"

Marja Braxton sat on one of the straight chairs. She folded her hands in her lap. "That is a real problem. When Gerda and Olina made my new dress, I had only seen the one style."

Olina stood looking out one of the windows at the back of the hotel. She could see a cluster of trees in the field. As the wind gently blew the branches, birds flitted in and out among the treetops, much as the birds at the farm had. It would be pleasant to watch them when she needed a break from the tedium of sewing. But maybe it wouldn't be quite so tedious when they used the treadle machine. She hoped not.

Olina turned back toward the other three women. "I have an idea, Mrs. Braxton."

"What?" Both women spoke in unison.

Marja laughed, then added, "You should call us Marja and Sophia. It would be a lot easier."

Sophia nodded. "I agree. Now Olina, dear, what was your idea?"

Olina spread the drawings out on the table. "You should pick your favorite drawing. Bring us the fabric you want to use. We'll start on that dress. Then you can choose the next favorite. That'll give you a little time to decide what fabric to make it from while we are working on the first. We'll make as many as we have time to this week, doing them one at a time like that."

Marja clapped her hands. "What a wonderful idea. Olina, you are a smart girl. I'm so glad you came to Minnesota." She pulled Olina into her arms and hugged her hard.

That hug reminded Olina of her mother. Maybe the people here did accept her for who she was. She could make a home for herself. Perhaps in time, she would find peace in her heart again.

When the men returned with the sewing machine, Olina was amazed. She had never seen anything like it. The black iron machine was attached to a small wooden table with iron legs. Under the table, a mesh contraption near the floor was attached to the machine above it. She had no idea how it could work, but she was eager to find out.

"Where is the manual?" Marja looked at the two men.

"Right here." Gustaf pulled a booklet from his back pocket and handed it to her. "Sorry I had to fold it, but I couldn't carry it and the machine at the same time."

Marja gave it to Olina. "Tonight you girls can read this and try to see how it works. Sophia and I will come in the morning for you to take her measurements. We'll bring the first fabric and notions." She clapped her hands. "Oh, I'm getting so excited."

"So am I," Sophia agreed as she took Marja's arm. "We need to go look at the fabric in the store. I have my eye on a couple of those drawings." Adolph quietly joined the two women as they walked down the hall, chattering about the different dresses.

Gustaf turned to Gerda, but he watched Olina out of the corner of his eye. "Could I take you and Olina to lunch downstairs?"

Gerda stood up. "Is it noon already? Where has the morning gone?"

"One, it took awhile to get to town." Gustaf counted on his fingers. "Two, we had to move your bags into your room. Three, we brought that heavy machine up two flights of stairs. That took time."

"Oh, you." Gerda playfully hit his arm. "That's not what I meant."

"I know." Gustaf laughed with her. Then he turned to Olina. "May I escort you to lunch?" When Olina nodded, he continued, "We'll let my sister come with us, if she'll behave herself."

Olina couldn't help herself. She burst out laughing with them. It felt so good to share a fun time. Maybe her heart could heal.

In the dining room, they were served a rich beef stew with hot corn bread slathered with fresh butter. While they were eating, several people from church stopped to visit. When they found out that the girls were staying in town for a week, they issued many invitations. Gerda and Olina wouldn't have to eat at the hotel very often, and they would have time to renew acquaintances and establish new friendships.

"I guess we'll not be sewing all the time." Gerda smiled at Olina.

"We need to sew a lot." Olina kept thinking about the money they would earn.

"I know that Marja and Sophia won't expect us to sew all our waking hours as if we were slaves."

When the waitress brought apple cobbler for dessert, she asked if they had heard about the brush arbor meeting that was going on that week. Olina didn't know what she was talking about, so Gustaf explained.

"We don't have many of these since we have our own church building. Traveling evangelists hold meetings in an open-air structure with a roof made out of tree limbs. I've heard that wonderful things happen at them." He got a faraway look on his face. "I've always wanted to attend one, and I hear this preacher has a powerful message." He looked back at the young women. "I think I'll come to town for the meeting tomorrow night." Turning toward Olina, he asked, "May I escort the two of you?"

Before Olina could decline, she heard Gerda accept with

eagerness. How could she not agree to accompany them? Maybe later she could think of a way out of it.

❧

Thank You, Father. On the way home late that afternoon, Gustaf was glad he had a reason to come to town tomorrow. He would have thought up some excuse, but this meeting was a good opportunity. He couldn't imagine worshiping out in the open like that. The services in their church were formal. This sounded as though it would be a chance to relax and worship with abandon. Of course, he sometimes did that when he was out working in the fields. He would take a break and sit under the shade and sing praises to the Lord. He had even been known to walk around praising the Lord with a loud voice, but only when he knew no one was near.

Gustaf had heard people talk about the old-time brush arbor meetings and how they would contain a lot of praise and worship; the ministers presented the gospel in a forceful, but understandable manner. Gustaf wanted to hear that kind of sermon. And he wanted to see Olina touched in a service. Maybe this meeting would be the time God could reach her in a new way, bringing healing to her wounded heart.

thirteen

When Marja and Sophia arrived the next morning, the four women spent an hour learning to use the sewing machine. It wasn't as hard as Olina had feared it would be. Then Olina and Gerda measured Sophia. After Sophia showed them which dress she wanted them to make out of the fabric they brought, she and Marja left the young women to their work.

Olina and Gerda cut out the bodice first. While Gerda cut out the rest of the dress, Olina started sewing the bodice, using the machine. By lunchtime, the dress was far enough along that the girls were sure they could finish it that day.

With a spring in their steps, Gerda and Olina started down the stairs to see what the restaurant was serving for lunch. Before they reached the bottom step, Merta Swenson came through the front door.

After greeting them, she asked, "Have you eaten yet?" When they shook their heads, she continued, "I want you to come to my house for lunch."

Merta served them chicken and dumplings, followed by gingerbread. This visit was the break from sewing that Gerda and Olina needed. After they were finished eating, Merta accompanied them on the walk back to the hotel.

"Remember how you said that you would like to move to town and be dressmakers here?" Merta asked as they reached the hotel.

"Yes," Gerda answered, and Olina nodded.

Merta pointed to a house down the road a ways, but still clearly visible from town. "The Winslow house is for sale. An older widow lived there, but her son wanted her to move to California with him, so she did."

Gerda studied the cottage for a minute. "From here, it looks as though it's in good shape."

"It is," Merta agreed. "Everyone in church made sure she was taken care of. Some of the men are still taking care of things at the house until it sells."

Olina could tell that it was a nice place and not at all small. She turned to Merta. "Do you have time to walk down there with us?"

"Please do." Gerda stepped off the wooden sidewalk. "We could look around, couldn't we?"

Merta took Olina's arm and pulled her with them. "It's not far. It won't take long."

The three young women walked along talking as they approached the cottage, set back from the road and surrounded by trees. When they reached the gate, Olina opened it and walked up on the front porch. It covered over half of the front of the house, with the front door at the end by whatever room projected beyond the porch. Olina stood in one of the two arches of the porch, which were held up by columns. She liked the shrubbery growing at the end and flowers beginning to bloom in the flower bed in front.

"I like this porch." Olina turned and looked back toward town. "It would be pleasant to sit out here in the cool of the evening." She slid down to sit on the top step. "I wish I had the money to buy this house, but I don't."

"Neither do I." Gerda sat beside her. "Maybe Father and Gustaf could work out a deal with the owner. I would like to move closer to town. This is far enough out from town to be away from all the noise, but close enough to be safe and convenient." She stood up and stepped away from the house. After turning, she looked up at the second story. "Merta, have you ever been inside?"

"Oh, yes." Merta joined her and looked up, too. "The second floor has two bedrooms in the front. There are two smaller rooms behind them. She used them for storage." Merta pointed to the room that was beside the porch. "That is the parlor. On the other side, she had a library. I think she used to be a schoolteacher, so she had lots of books. Behind those two rooms are a kitchen, with a large area for a table and chairs, and a big pantry."

Olina stood up and looked back toward town. "It sounds perfect. If only. . ."

"We need to pray about this. Maybe the Lord wants us here." Gerda took hold of both Olina's hand and Merta's. Then she asked God to provide a way. . .if He wanted them to live in this house.

❧

Just as Gerda and Olina sewed the last button on the dress, a knock sounded at the door.

"That must be Sophia." Olina was glad for the opportunity to get up and move around. She stretched her arms over her head for a minute before she opened the door. "You're just in ti—" She was startled and stopped with a gasp.

"Well, what a welcome." Gustaf's laughing gaze met her startled one. "I didn't know you were expecting me."

Olina could feel her cheeks redden. She wanted to hide them, but she couldn't look away from him. She liked to see the merriment in his eyes. Was that something more? Whatever could it be? She shook her head. Why did Gustaf have this effect on her? Maybe it was because she had not expected to see him filling her doorway.

"We thought you were Sophia." Gerda jumped up and came over to hug her brother. "But I'm glad you're here, even though I don't know why." She stepped back. "Come in."

Gustaf seemed to fill the room, too. Olina turned back to the dress they had dropped in a heap on the bed. She picked it up and started folding it as she listened to Gustaf and Gerda.

"Do I have to have a reason to come see my little sister?" With his finger, he flicked a curl that was drooping on her forehead.

Gerda playfully hit him on the arm. "You are a big tease. Isn't that right, Olina?"

Olina looked at Gerda. "Yes, he does tease a lot."

"So what brings you to town?" Gerda came over to help Olina finish folding the dress.

"Remember yesterday at lunch, I said I would be coming into town for the brush arbor meeting." Gustaf looked from Gerda to Olina. "I came a little early. I wanted to check on the two of you so I can assure Father that you're all right."

Gerda rolled her eyes.

"I thought maybe you two lovely ladies would join me for dinner before the meeting." Gustaf looked at Olina, waiting for her to answer.

They did have to eat. Olina picked up the dress and moved it to the table. With her back turned from Gustaf, she answered, "We could do that."

All afternoon Olina and Gerda had been smelling roast beef cooking. "I think we are having roast." Olina sniffed the air. "It smells like they are cooking yeast rolls. It should be good."

Their meal was a congenial affair. Gustaf and Gerda kept up a lively conversation. Although Olina was quieter, she enjoyed listening to them.

"Gustaf." Gerda sounded excited. "Merta, Olina, and I went to the Winslow house today."

Gustaf swallowed a mouthful. "Why did you do that?"

"It's for sale." Gerda buttered a hot roll.

Gustaf looked at Gerda, then at Olina. "Why would you be

interested in a house that's for sale?"

"I know that we don't have the money to buy it." Gerda put down the roll and clasped her hands in her lap. "But Olina and I would like to move closer to town."

Gustaf raised his eyebrows. Olina looked down at her plate, but she peeked at Gustaf through her eyelashes. He turned toward Gerda.

"Why is that?"

"Oh, Gustaf." Gerda placed her forearms on the table and eagerly leaned toward him. "There's no dressmaker in Litchfield. Olina and I think we could make a living here."

Gustaf looked thoughtful. "You might be able to."

"It's no use to think about it though." Gerda sighed and picked up her forgotten roll. "Father would never let us do it. But the house would be perfect for us. The woman who lived there was a teacher, and she had a library with lots of windows. That room would make a wonderful workroom for us."

Just then the waitress brought their dessert to them. In a moment, she returned with a large pitcher of water to refill their glasses and a cup of coffee for Gustaf.

When they had finished eating rice pudding with raisins and cinnamon, Gerda wiped her mouth with the napkin. "I would like to go to the meeting with you, Gustaf."

"I had hoped you would say that." He turned toward Olina. "What about you?"

"Of course she'll go. She won't want to sit alone in the hotel room." Gerda got up from her chair. "We need to go freshen up before we leave. What time does it start?"

"You have plenty of time." Gustaf helped Olina push her chair away from the table. He walked them into the lobby. As he watched the two go up the stairs, he called after them, "I'll be waiting right here for you."

When the young women came back down the stairs, August

had joined Gustaf. The two men looked as if they were praying together. Surely they weren't doing that right there in the lobby of the hotel. They must be having a private conversation.

"Wonderful." Gerda pulled Olina across the lobby. "August is here, too."

The two men glanced up when they heard Gerda's exclamation. August grabbed her in a bear hug and swung her feet off the floor. When he put her down, he turned toward Olina. "You look nice tonight. I'm glad Gustaf talked me into going with the three of you."

Olina looked at Gustaf. Once again, she felt a blush rise to color her cheeks. She had known other women who didn't turn red every time a man looked at them. Why couldn't she be like them?

The evening was cool but pleasant when they arrived at the structure covered with fresh branches. Olina hoped that the four of them would sit on the back bench, but Gustaf led them down the center aisle. He stopped about halfway between the back and the front. He motioned for August, Gerda, and Olina to precede him on the bench, leaving him sitting on the aisle. He probably needed to sit there so he would have somewhere to put his long legs. The benches weren't far apart.

Olina wondered if many people would come to the meeting. Soon most of the benches were full, and men stood outside the arbor, looking in. Olina was glad. At least they wouldn't be conspicuous. When everyone was crowded into the structure, it warmed up a bit.

A large man with snow-white hair stood from the front bench and stepped onto the short platform. When he turned around, he unbuttoned his black frock coat and raised his hands. All talking ceased. His booming voice led in an opening prayer. Olina had never heard a prayer like the one he prayed. He sounded as if God was his friend, not just someone who lived in heaven and kept His distance. In the Swedish church they attended here, as well as the church back in Sweden, God had seemed far from Olina.

She used to love Him. She had liked learning about Him, but she hadn't thought of Him as a friend. When this man said "Father," his voice held love and warmth, not just awe. Olina didn't know what to think about that.

After the man finished praying, he started singing a song Olina had never heard before. However, the words and the music touched something in her that she had been hiding. The first line, "Love divine, all loves excelling, Joy of heaven to earth come down," awakened a longing. Olina felt uncomfortable. If she had been sitting on the back bench, she would have slipped out and returned to the hotel room. The longer the singing continued, the more uncomfortable she became. Her mother had always told her not to squirm in church, but the wooden bench was hard even through the layers of her clothing.

When the first song ended, the leader started another, without announcing what it would be. That didn't bother the other people. By the second word, most of them were singing with him.

Olina didn't sing along. She had never heard this song, either. She didn't want to "survey the wondrous cross." Olina didn't want to think about Jesus dying for her. She didn't want to think that He loved her. By now she was fidgeting a lot. Maybe she could tell Gerda that she needed to use the necessary.

When the singer started the third song and everyone joined in, Olina couldn't shut the words out of her mind. "Amazing Grace, how sweet the sound." How she would like to believe in that amazing grace, but she knew that God had not protected her from grievous hurt.

≈

Gustaf was attuned to Olina's every move. He could tell that she was uncomfortable. Maybe it would have been better not to bring her. He and August had prayed for Olina while they waited for the two young women to come down to the lobby. Perhaps it wasn't the time for God to speak to her yet.

Gustaf had been humming along after he caught on to the melody of the songs. The words had gone right to his heart, making it joyful, but that didn't seem to be the case with Olina. Maybe he should offer to walk her back to the hotel. But something stopped him from asking her.

❧

The last song started. *Holy Spirit, Truth divine, dawn upon this soul of mine; Word of God and inward light, wake my spirit, clear my sight.*

Those words calmed Olina. Could the Spirit of God clear her sight? By the time the song ended, she had stopped fidgeting. She let the music pour over her, hoping it would indeed bring her lasting peace. But how could she trust God?

When the singer finished, he returned to his seat on the front bench, and another man stepped onto the platform. He was a small, wiry man carrying a big black Bible under his arm. He turned and looked out across the group that was gathered. It seemed to Olina that his gaze stopped when he reached her. For a moment suspended in time, he continued to look at her before he continued on across the crowd. She felt as if he could see everything in her heart. Why was he interested in her?

He stood there for several moments. The crowd was quiet except for a mother in the back, shushing her fussy baby. After the long pause, the preacher cleared his throat, pulled a large white handkerchief from his pocket, and mopped beads of perspiration from his forehead. Then he opened the Bible near the middle.

"I'm going to read to you from the book of Jeremiah, the

twenty-ninth chapter, verses eleven through thirteen." Once more, he cleared his throat before continuing. " 'For I know the thoughts that I think toward you, saith the Lord, thoughts of peace, and not of evil, to give you an expected end. Then shall ye call upon me, and ye shall go and pray unto me, and I will hearken unto you. And ye shall seek me, and find me, when ye shall search for me with all your heart.' "

When he once again cleared his throat, the singer moved to the platform and handed the preacher a tin cup of water. After taking a swig, he gave it back to the man with a whisper of thanks. "I'm also going to read the first part of the fourteenth verse: 'And I will be found of you, saith the Lord.' "

Olina didn't remember those words from the Bible. Maybe it was because she didn't really like the Old Testament. It was harder for her to understand than the New Testament. She hadn't paid much attention when Fader read to the family from the Old Testament. But she thought she would have remembered those words. They had lodged in her heart after the preacher read them.

"I believe God is talking about His plans for us." The preacher closed the Bible and walked back and forth across the small platform. "God has plans for us, and they are plans that are good, not bad. He knows what He wants to happen in our lives. Sometimes it doesn't seem that way, but in the end, the good He intends will come to pass."

Could this be true? Olina didn't know. She only knew that God had allowed so much to happen to her. If He wanted good to come from it, when was it going to happen? Olina didn't hear any more of the preacher's sermon, but his opening words kept ringing through her heart and mind. God had plans for her good. Did He? Could she trust Him to bring them about?

fourteen

When Sophia and Marja came to the hotel late Monday afternoon, Olina and Gerda had finished two dresses that day. These would be the last, since Sophia and Adolph were leaving on the train Tuesday morning. Because they had been so busy, the week had flown by.

On Wednesday and Thursday, Olina and Gerda had made one dress per day. Once they became used to the sewing machine, everything went more quickly. Starting on Friday, they were able to finish two dresses per day. They had taken turns with each new dress. On one, Gerda cut the dress out while Olina sewed the pieces together. On the next one, they switched places. That way they both learned to use the machine. They shared the handwork, sewing on buttons and hemming.

"I can hardly believe I have eight new dresses at one time. These will last me for years." Sophia held up the light blue dimity, and its full skirt spread around her. "I've never had such a fine wardrobe as this." Her smile warmed Olina's heart. "What are you girls doing tonight?"

Olina looked at Gerda, who was making a bundle of the fabric scraps. She would take them home so her mother could use them in a quilt. "We'll be packing, getting ready for Gustaf to come for us tomorrow morning."

Sophia glanced down at the dress again. "I want to wear this before I leave town. Adolph and I would like to have you girls as our guests for dinner tonight."

Marja clapped her hands. "What a wonderful idea. We

could all eat together."

"Of course," Sophia agreed. "It can be a dinner party. I'll check with the hotel to see if we can get festive food for tonight."

Sophia and Marja gathered up their things. They had started toward the door when Sophia turned back.

"I almost forgot to give you this." She opened her reticule and pulled a sealed envelope from it, thrusting it into Olina's hands. "I've put a little bonus in this along with what I agreed to pay you. You've done such a good job."

Before the young women could demur, Marja and Sophia had bustled out the door, chattering about the plans for the evening.

Gerda looked at Olina, who was using both hands to test the weight of the envelope. Olina could tell that it held quite a bit of money.

"Well, look at it, Olina." Gerda was anxious.

Olina was careful not to tear the paper as she looked inside. Several greenbacks spilled from the envelope onto the bed. Olina dumped the rest and sat beside the pile to divide it into two stacks. She had never seen that much money at one time in her whole life. At first, she just sat and looked at it. *What a blessing!* Now why did she think that? Did she still believe in blessings?

Since the first night of the brush arbor meetings, Olina had pondered the words of the evangelist. She wanted to read the words he shared from the Bible in her mother tongue, but she had not brought her Bible with her. Because of what her father had told her, she had left it at her aunt's house. After that Wednesday night meeting, Olina had written her aunt a letter, asking her to send the Bible to America. She wanted to wait to face the words until it came, but they kept popping into her head at the oddest times.

The preacher had said things on Thursday and Friday night

that piqued her interest, but none as strongly as that first night. Did God have plans for her? If so, what were they?

"This is a lot of money." Gerda's comment interrupted Olina's musings.

"Yes, it is." Olina still stared at the two piles.

Gerda sat on the bed across from Olina, the money between them. "I have an idea."

Olina looked up at Gerda. "What?"

"Do you remember how much Marja said the sewing machine cost?"

Olina nodded.

"Look at all this." Gerda picked up her share of the bounty and let it drift back to the bed. "If we put our shares together, we could buy that machine and still have plenty of money left."

Olina's eyes widened as she looked at her friend. She hadn't even thought about anything like that. Maybe Gerda's idea was a good one.

"Remember at church?" Gerda started stacking her money in a neat pile. "When the other women saw Marja's and Sophia's new dresses, we got orders from four other women."

Olina was getting interested. "We could make those dresses much faster with the machine." She walked over to the piece of equipment and rubbed her hand over the wooden table that held the machine head. "If we are going to be dressmakers, we need this."

Gerda joined her. "It would be wonderful if somehow we could move to the house we saw and sew from there." She got a dreamy look in her eyes. "We did pray and ask God to provide for us. Look what He has already provided."

Olina could only agree. Maybe, just maybe, she had been wrong, and God had not deserted her as she had thought.

The party that evening was festive. The glow of candlelight

glistened from polished silver and crystal goblets, and a floral centerpiece graced the table. Instead of the roast beef most people were having for dinner, they each had a tender steak, surrounded by fresh vegetables. The dainty rolls were fluffy and browned to perfection. Dessert was a light chocolate pastry with a custard filling. Olina had never tasted anything like it.

While the guests enjoyed their meals, several people came over to talk to Olina and Gerda. Some of them were visiting with Sophia and Adolph before they went back to Denver. Other couples came for the wives to look at the dresses all four women wore. Olina and Gerda had worn the pastel silk frocks they had made before they had come to town to sew for Sophia. Three more women wanted to talk to them about making them dresses.

"Marja," Gerda said as they were getting ready to go up to their rooms. "You said that Johan would pick up the sewing machine in the morning when we are getting ready to leave."

"Yes, Dear, I hope that's all right." Marja patted Gerda on the arm.

"Well, Olina and I have decided that we want to buy the machine with the money we made this week."

Marja clapped her hands. "What a wonderful idea." Then she put her arms around both young women. "You have so many more dresses to make already."

The three women started up the staircase. "We thought it would be a good investment," Olina added.

৶

"I'm glad Johan came to help me carry that heavy machine down to the wagon." Gustaf made a clucking sound to the horses, and they started out of town. "Here I thought I had carried it on those stairs for the last time." He chuckled. "It's a good thing we needed to pick up some feed for the horses. If not, I would have brought the buggy, not the wagon."

Gerda was seated between Gustaf and Olina on the wagon seat. She poked Olina with her elbow. "He always has something to complain about, doesn't he?" The young women giggled. "I think he likes helping us."

Olina peeked around Gerda to see that Gustaf was looking right at her. "Do you agree?" he asked.

Goose bumps ran up her arms. "I think. . ." Olina swallowed and looked away.

"What do you think, Olina?" Gerda seemed oblivious to the charge in the air.

"I think that Gustaf does like to help. . .us." Olina ducked her head. "But I don't think he complains much. At least I don't hear him."

When a robust laugh burst from Gustaf, another feeling ran up Olina's spine. She was not sure what it was, but she knew that she liked to hear Gustaf's hearty laugh. It sounded musical to her, like the symphony she and Tant Olga attended before she came to America—rich, full, and heartwarming. At least it warmed her heart today. But it wasn't just the laugh. That was only part of what warmed her heart. After all, she and Gerda really became professional dressmakers when they bought that treadle sewing machine. Her life was taking shape. It had a purpose now.

Ingrid Nilsson prepared a special feast to celebrate the return of the young women. Even August came home to have dinner with them. He said that Gustaf invited him when he came to town to pick them up. The meal was a lively, happy time, with much talking and teasing among the Nilsson family. However, Olina remained silent, listening to the others and remembering such evenings with her family back in Sweden. The times she thought of them were not as often, but since writing the letter to Tant Olga, Olina couldn't get them off her mind. A veritable smorgasbord of thoughts tumbled through her head.

Dressmaking. The house on the edge of town. Her family. In the midst of all those thoughts, Gustaf's face often appeared.

"Isn't that right, Olina?" Gerda's voice penetrated her reverie.

Olina looked at her friend.

"I was telling Father about all the women who want us to make dresses for them." Gerda smiled at Olina.

"Oh, yes. It's amazing. Even with the sewing machine, we will be busy for a couple of weeks." Olina could feel a blush creeping up her neck. She should pay attention to what the others were saying.

"By the time we're finished," Gerda added, "perhaps more women will want our dresses."

"What sewing machine?" Mr. Nilsson had a puzzled expression.

Olina looked at Gerda, wondering if she shouldn't have said anything about the machine. She assumed that Mr. Nilsson knew about it by now.

"Olina and I used some of the money we made this week to buy the treadle sewing machine Mrs. Braxton let us use to make her sister-in-law's dresses." Gerda smiled at her father.

Olina noticed that the puzzlement in his face softened. "Since we have so many other dresses to make, it was a good investment."

Mr. Nilsson's face softened even more. "That is so, for sure. You girls used your heads." He took another bite of creamy mashed potatoes. "Ja, it was a good investment."

"I made a good investment this week, too." Everyone stopped eating and looked at Gustaf as he continued. "Father, remember the Winslow house right outside town?" He waited for his father to nod. "Brian Winslow moved to California."

"I remember hearing that," Mr. Nilsson said.

Mrs. Nilsson passed the fried chicken to August, who didn't

have any more on his plate. "I heard that he took his mother with him."

"He did." Gerda picked up another hot roll and buttered it.

Olina wondered where this discussion was headed. She didn't have to wait long to find out.

Gustaf put his fork on his plate and tented his fingers over it. "The Winslow house was for sale. I talked to their lawyer last week. This morning I signed the papers making the house mine."

Olina and Gerda looked at each other with stunned expressions. Gustaf had bought their house. The house they had prayed for God to find a way for them to rent. A plan was forming in Olina's mind, and she could tell that Gerda's thoughts were running along the same lines. Maybe. But it could never be. Mr. Nilsson wouldn't agree to let two young women live alone, even though it was near town.

"Gustaf." Mr. Nilsson laid his fork down and looked at his son. "Why did you buy the house?"

Gustaf looked at his father, man to man. "The price was reasonable, and I had more than enough money saved. Some day, I may want to live there with my wife."

"Son, you know that you'll always have a home here on the farm."

Gustaf smiled. "I know that. But when I marry, we might want to live closer to town. It wouldn't mean that I couldn't work the farm. It's not that far from here."

August couldn't let that comment pass. "Just when are you planning on getting married?" He jabbed Gustaf in the ribs, laughing.

Gustaf ignored the teasing. "I don't know when God will have me marry, but I know He doesn't want me to be a solitary man all my life."

He looked at Olina when he made that solemn declaration.

Her heart began to beat double time at the sound of his voice and the words he said.

"What will you do with the house right now?" Mr. Nilsson took the conversation back to the heart of the matter. "It isn't good for a house to sit empty for long."

"I know that." With a smile, Gustaf glanced at Gerda and then Olina. "Since the girls have several clients in town, they could live in the house."

Olina expected a negative exclamation from Mr. Nilsson about that statement. Her father would have vehemently denied the request. But the room was silent except for August's fork scraping on his plate. Everyone else in the room had stopped eating. The silence lengthened, while Olina held her breath.

Finally Mr. Nilsson answered Gustaf. "I'm not sure I like that idea. The girls are under my protection, and I don't want anything happening to them."

"Father, I know that." Gustaf once more leaned his fore-arms on the table with his fingers tented over his plate. "Look at Gerda and Olina. They aren't girls. They are women."

Mr. Nilsson looked at Olina first, then turned his attention toward his daughter. Olina could tell that he was seeing them differently than he ever had before.

"You're right, my son, but they still need protection."

Gustaf nodded. "That can be arranged. Several men in the church have been looking after the property since the Winslows left. I'm sure they would help look after the young women."

It sounded to Olina as if Gustaf emphasized the words *young women*.

August put his fork down. "I could check on them every day, too, Father. It would be nice to have part of the family living closer to me."

"I know we don't have locks on this house," Gustaf contin-ued, "but I had locks installed on that one. It would make

Gerda and Olina feel safer at night."

August looked at Gerda with a smile. "I could make a big dinner bell for the girls to hang outside. Then if they need help, they can ring it. I could hear it from where I work and where I live."

Mr. Nilsson looked around the table at each of his children. "You have all given convincing arguments." Then he looked at Olina. "Is this what you would like to do, Olina?"

A large lump had grown in her throat, and she couldn't get any words around it, so she nodded. Mr. Nilsson studied her face as if he were trying to read her thoughts. Then he picked up his fork. "Let's finish this wonderful meal, so we can have a piece of that apple pie I smelled as I came into the house. I'll think on this discussion and give you my decision in the morning."

fifteen

Gustaf knew that his father was a fair man with a strong sense of responsibility for his family. He would pray about the decision he had to make before morning.

Gustaf had prayed before he bought the house. God hadn't given him that check in his spirit that helped keep him from making wrong decisions. He felt complete peace about buying the property and couldn't help thinking about the possibility that he would one day live there with Olina as his wife. The house was perfect for a newlywed couple. Olina could continue to be a dressmaker, if she wanted to. When God blessed their marriage with children, he would build onto the house to accommodate however many children God blessed them with. There was plenty of room for expansion.

He imagined little girls with blond curls blowing in the wind as they played in the yard or even swung from limbs of trees. When they were younger, Gerda and Olina had climbed trees right along with their brothers. His sons would accompany him to the farm to help their grandfather.

What was he thinking? In his mind, he had children when he didn't even know whether Olina would ever forgive him. If she did, she might never come to love him as he already loved her. He needed to turn his thoughts to more profitable pursuits.

Gustaf got on his knees with his Bible open on the bed beside him. He prayed for a few minutes. Then he read a passage of Scripture about God hearing and answering prayers before he returned to his supplications. After over an hour spent in the presence of his heavenly Father, peace descended over Gustaf's soul. He knew that no matter what his earthly father decided, it would be the will of the heavenly Father. Clothed in that peace, Gustaf climbed into his bed and fell into a deep, restful sleep.

❧

Olina paced the floor of her room, thinking about the discussion at dinner. Could it be possible that Mr. Nilsson would let them move to the house?

Trust Me, Olina. The voice sounded in her mind. A voice that was getting harder to ignore since the first night at the brush arbor meeting. Did God have a plan for her? Did it include living in the house? Olina never imagined that it would be so simple to establish herself as a dressmaker. Had God been a part of that?

She wanted to pray for Mr. Nilsson as he made the decision, but it had been a long time since she trusted God enough to ask Him for anything. She knew that Gerda was probably praying right now, if she hadn't already gone to sleep. Maybe even Gustaf was talking to God about his father's decision. Olina hoped so. Gerda and Gustaf still trusted God. He would listen to them.

I will listen to you, too, Olina.

Olina wished that were true, but she had ignored God for so long, how could He want to hear what she said?

When Olina awoke, she could tell that she had overslept. The sun, streaming through her window, was too high in the sky for it to be early morning. She quickly dressed and went downstairs to the kitchen, where she was met by the smells of bacon and biscuits.

"I'm so sorry I overslept."

Mrs. Nilsson turned at the sound of Olina's voice. "That's all right, Olina. We decided to let you sleep until you awoke. Gerda heard you moving around in your room late into the night."

Olina frowned. "I didn't want to disturb anyone."

Mrs. Nilsson put her arms around Olina and pulled her into a maternal hug. "Olina, Dear, you didn't disturb anyone. I think Gerda was awake a long time, too. She was probably praying about her father's decision." She patted Olina's arm before turning back to the skillet on the wood stove. "I've kept the bacon and biscuits warm. Would you like one egg or two?"

"Only one, but let me cook it." Olina started toward the extra apron hanging on the hook beside the back door.

"No, please let me do this for you." Mrs. Nilsson broke an egg into the skillet. She started basting the egg with the warm bacon grease as she continued. "After all, I won't be cooking for you much longer."

Olina sat down hard in the chair she had pulled out from the table. "Do you mean what I think you mean?" She was afraid to believe what she had heard.

"Yes, Dear. Bennel said that you and Gerda could move into Gustaf's house."

Olina was speechless. It was too wonderful to imagine. Was this part of God's plans for her? Whether it was or not, Olina was ecstatic. She couldn't hold back a giggle that bubbled from deep within.

"I'm glad that makes you happy." Mrs. Nilsson set the plate of food in front of Olina. "Now eat up. Gustaf and Gerda are finishing the chores, so the three of you can look at the house. They want to see what needs to be done to get it ready for you to move in."

Olina was so excited that she thought she couldn't eat, but when she took the first bite of the light fluffy bread, it whetted her appetite. By the time Gerda and Gustaf came in from outdoors, she had cleaned up everything on her plate.

Gerda burst through the back door like a whirlwind. "Olina, has Mother told you?" When Olina nodded, she continued.

"Isn't it wonderful?" She ran around the table and pulled Olina up into a hug. Olina felt as if Gerda were cutting her in two with her strong arms, but she hugged Gerda back just as hard.

Gustaf soon followed Gerda into the kitchen. "If you girls. . . young women. . .would get ready, we'll be off to town."

Gerda and Olina turned to look at him. His smile was as big as theirs.

"We'll be ready in ten minutes. Right, Olina?" Gerda hurried out into the hall.

Olina couldn't tear her gaze from Gustaf. He looked so strong and masculine. The freshness of the warm summer morning surrounded him, and his eyes communicated something to her soul. She didn't know, or recognize, what it was, but she liked it. It made her feel fresh and warm as the morning.

❧

While Gustaf unlocked the front door of his house, Olina stood on the porch, looking out toward the road. Everything around them was in the full bloom of summer. Trees were clothed in various shades of green above their brown or gray trunks. Birds were singing in some of the trees. Prairie grasses, blowing in the wind, were dotted with white, pink, and yellow wild flowers. When she looked down the road to her right, Litchfield looked rooted in the prairie as much as the trees were. It felt as if it were part of the landscape, a close neighbor to keep the house from being lonely. Taking a deep breath of the fresh air, Olina let out a sigh of contentment. This would soon be her home. But she had to ask Gustaf one question.

Olina turned to look toward him, only to find him smiling at her. Gerda had already entered the house.

"So, how much rent are you going to charge us?"

The look that passed over his face was one of hurt, then

understanding. "I won't charge rent to anyone in the family."

"Oh, but I'm not—"

Before Olina could finish, Gustaf interrupted with a teasing comment as he walked over to stand in front of her. "But you can cook me a hot meal every once in awhile. That would be a fair rent."

Olina had to look up to meet the challenge in his face. "Why would you need a hot meal when your mother cooks so well?"

Her question, which had started on a strong note, ended with a soft breathy word. Gustaf leaned closer as if he were having a hard time hearing her. Olina didn't know whether to step back or stay where she was. He was entirely too close for comfort. But she would not allow him to cause her to move.

"Does that mean I can't enjoy another woman's cooking?"

There he was emphasizing the word *woman* again. Olina liked the fact that he knew she was a woman, but that knowledge caused unfamiliar feelings within her. She couldn't decide whether they were comfortable feelings or not.

His gaze held hers, and time stood still. The fragrance of soap and something else that Olina couldn't define enveloped her in a world inhabited by the two of them. Olina couldn't ever remember any man she had known smelling quite like that. Sweat, she had smelled, and soap, but not this masculine aroma. It was heady and scary at the same time.

Gustaf reached toward her when the sound of Gerda's voice came from inside the house. "Olina, look. The house has furniture in almost every room."

Gustaf pulled back as Olina turned toward the door.

"Yes, there was too much furniture to take to California, so they left most of it. If the person who bought the house didn't want the furnishings, they would have been sold at an auction for the Winslows. I thought we could use most of it."

Olina was still dazed by what had happened on the porch, but she looked around her, trying to get her bearings back. The Chesterfield in the parlor looked to be in good condition. She decided to try it out. It might help to sit for a minute. While she walked to the sofa, she looked at the chairs and tables arranged around the room. A large rug covered the floor. The room had a homey feel.

Olina dropped onto the comfortable sofa. She ran her finger across the table that sat beside it.

"Merta swept and dusted the house for me yesterday while I was in town." Olina raised her head at the sound of Gustaf's voice from the doorway. Now that she was across the room from him, she had her equilibrium back.

"That was nice." Olina didn't look into Gustaf's eyes. She focused on the wall beside the door.

"I told her someone might be moving in pretty soon." Gustaf looked at the wall, too. "Do you think we should put up new wallpaper?"

Gerda walked up behind him. "This wallpaper is lovely. Isn't it, Olina?"

Olina nodded, for the first time noticing the ivy pattern. "Everything is wonderful."

Gustaf stepped into the room. "Do you think the curtains need washing?"

Gerda walked over and lifted the edge of one. "Of course they do. They'll be filled with dust. Come, Olina. Let me show you the rest of the house."

After the tour, the trio decided to have a workday the next day. They would bring all the things needed to wash the curtains in the house. Their search of the cupboards revealed that there were enough dishes, pots and pans, and utensils for the young women to set up housekeeping. They could add to them as needed. One of the closets even held bed linens. They would want to wash them when they washed the curtains.

The room that Mrs. Winslow used as a library had shelves on two walls and windows on the other two. It would be ideal for the sewing room. They could utilize the shelves to showcase fabrics and notions, and the windows gave it a light, airy feeling. Since the room contained no furniture, there was plenty of space for a cutting table, the sewing machine, and whatever chairs Gerda and Olina needed in their business. It might take them a little time to completely furnish it as they would like, but the possibilities made both girls excited.

"It won't take long to get the house ready to move in," Gerda gushed. "One or two workdays, and we'll be living here."

She hugged Olina hard again. Olina felt like dancing as she had when she was an excited little girl. But today she was no longer a girl. She must act as a woman would. She never wanted Gustaf to think of her as a little girl again.

❧

The whole family decided to participate in the workday at Gustaf's house. Even August took the day off from the blacksmith's. Mrs. Nilsson decided to cook dinner at the house, and Mr. Nilsson wanted to check everything out before Gerda and Olina moved in.

After chores were finished, they piled into the wagon. Mrs. Nilsson sat on the seat between Mr. Nilsson and Gustaf. Gerda and Olina sat in the back of the wagon, surrounded by cleaning supplies and various items they were taking to the house.

When they stopped the wagon, they sat for a minute while Mr. and Mrs. Nilsson looked at the cottage and its surroundings.

Mrs. Nilsson was the first to break the silence. "Oh, Gustaf, I like it. It's so pretty from the outside."

Mr. Nilsson nodded his agreement before he stepped to the ground. While he was helping his wife out of the wagon, August called to them from down the road toward town.

They all pitched in and soon the windows were open wide, letting in the summer breeze to air out all the rooms. While the women put water on to boil, the men took down the curtains. August tested the clothesline to make sure it was stable. Then he used a wet rag to wipe the dust off the wire before the women hung clean items over it.

When the first load of water was hot, Mrs. Nilsson put another pot on the back of the stove to heat. She placed the pot of beef stew that she had brought from home on the front of the stove to heat for lunch.

About the time they were going to stop to eat, Merta pulled up in her buggy. Two other women from the church were with her. They brought hot corn bread and butter, lemonade, and a pound cake. The women insisted on taking over the work in the kitchen, making Ingrid sit down and rest while they served everyone.

Lunch was like a party to Olina. She enjoyed having Merta there, but she also got to know the other two women better.

"Are you a good cook?" August asked Olina. "I've eaten some things that Gerda made that weren't so good."

Gerda, who was sitting beside him, hit him playfully on the arm. "That was a long time ago."

"Yes, both Mother and Tant Olga insisted that I learn to cook." Olina smiled at August. "Maybe you could eat with us sometime, since we're so close now."

"That would be wonderful," Gerda exclaimed. "I would love to fix you breakfast and dinner every day. I'm not sure about lunch every day, though. We'll be busy in the daytime. We have a lot of orders to fill."

"I might take you up on that." August smiled as if he had been given a special present.

And I might take you up on it sometime, too. For the first time in his life, Gustaf envied his brother.

sixteen

It took only one day to finish getting the cottage ready, so Gerda and Olina planned to move on Friday. Mrs. Nilsson gathered some of her kitchen items to add to the things left in the house. She also packed a few towels, more sheets, and two good goose-down pillows.

With Gerda and Olina in her bedroom, she opened the large cedar chest. Inside were a number of handmade quilts. She let each of the young women pick two for their own beds. While adding some cutwork kitchen towels and crocheted doilies to the growing stack, she furtively wiped a tear from the corner of her eye, but Olina noticed the movement.

Perhaps her own mother had shed tears about her daughter leaving home. For a moment, Olina's heart yearned to see her mother's dear face. *Please, Gud, let me see Mor again, at least once.* After she had that thought, Olina realized that it was a prayer.

When they had unloaded the first wagon full of things at the house, Gustaf and his father returned to the farm to bring another load. Olina was surprised that there was more than would fill one wagon. In addition to her hand luggage, she had brought two trunks full of things with her when she moved from Sweden. Gerda had a lifetime of possessions to move. She didn't seem to be leaving anything at her parents' home.

Mrs. Nilsson insisted on giving a large table to Gerda and Olina for them to use in the sewing room. Besides that, she gave them two rocking chairs that were in the attic of the farmhouse, along with two straight chairs. Olina couldn't imagine that they would need anything else at their new home. Her small hoard of money wouldn't have to be used for furnishings. That was a blessing.

When the men returned and unloaded the wagon the second time, Merta arrived. She said that some of the women had prepared lunch for them. They had the table set at Merta's house waiting for them to come.

"We can't possibly go looking like this." Olina pushed a stray curl back under the scarf she had tied around her head.

"Yes, you can." Gustaf touched her cheek with one finger, rubbing at a spot. "You have some dust on your face, but it won't take you long to clean up."

Olina turned away to hide the blush she could feel staining her cheeks. More than her cheek was affected by the touch of his finger.

"Of course not," Gerda agreed. After filling a white pitcher with a rose pattern on the side, she picked up the matching bowl and invited her mother to accompany her to her bedroom to freshen up.

Olina soon followed with a pure white bowl and pitcher of fresh water for her own bedroom. Setting it on the washstand, she peered into the looking glass on the wall above it. After removing the scarf, she fluffed her hair with her brush and pulled it back, tying it at the nape of her neck with the scarf. That would have to do. She didn't have time to put it up properly.

Olina was descending the stairs when Gustaf returned from washing at the pump in the kitchen. He caught his breath when he looked up at her. He hadn't seen her like that since she arrived in America. Even though her hair was tied back, curls cascaded past her waist. It reminded him of the bubbling waterfall on the farm in Sweden, as it sparkled in the sun. He had seen her many times back in Sweden. When she hadn't had her hair in braids as a young girl, she wore it tied back, but he didn't remember it like this. Gustaf wished he had the right to run his fingers through the silky-looking strands. He had to just imagine what they would feel like curled around his fingers.

"Is everyone ready?" His father's voice sounded from behind him.

Gustaf was glad that his father hadn't been watching his face. He knew Gustaf too well, and he might realize what Gustaf was thinking. Gustaf wasn't ready to discuss his feelings for Olina with anyone, especially not his father.

While they were eating, the women from church asked if there was anything else they could do to help Gerda and Olina get settled in the Winslow house.

"I guess it's no longer the Winslow house." Gustaf couldn't keep the pride out of his voice. "From now on, it will be the Nilsson house."

Olina knew what he was saying, but she was not a Nilsson. It felt different to be living in a Nilsson house when Gustaf owned it instead of his father, but she wasn't yet ready to explore the reason.

Two of the women had talked to Gerda and Olina about sewing for them. They made arrangements to bring fabric to the cottage on Monday, so that Gerda and Olina could get started making their dresses. Olina felt so professional. She thought Gerda felt the same, because they shared a secret smile across the table.

It didn't take long for Gerda and Olina to settle into a routine. In the mornings, after doing whatever cleaning the house needed, they started sewing on dresses for customers. Working together, they had no trouble finishing a dress, sometimes more, in a day. As women began wearing their new frocks, more were ordered, both by the same women and others. By the end of the first month they lived in the house, their business was thriving.

August quickly formed the habit of eating breakfast with the young women. Sometimes when they were busy, he would invite them to join him for lunch at his boardinghouse. The food there was good, and it kept Gerda and Olina from having to take time to cook. They took turns fixing dinner.

It soon became apparent that Gustaf meant what he said about the rent being a hot meal. It wasn't at all unusual for him to arrive in town to share lunch or dinner with them four or more times a week. Not that Olina minded. It was pleasant to have him around. When he was there, he checked to see if there were any repairs that needed to be done at the house.

❧

Two months had passed when Gustaf arrived carrying a package. "Olina, I have something for you." He strode into the sewing room and stopped short. She was standing on a straight chair, trying to reach something on a high shelf. "What do you think you are doing?" His voice exploded.

The loudness and harshness must have startled Olina because she lost her balance, teetering on the chair before her feet flew out from under her. Gustaf hurled the package to the floor and lunged toward her, barely catching her. He pulled her hard against his heaving chest. What a scare she had given him. He didn't realize how hard he was clutching her to himself until he heard her soft sob. That sound cut right to his heart.

Gustaf loosened his hold, cradling her gently against his still pounding heart. "I'm so sorry. I didn't mean to hurt you."

Olina hiccoughed. "You scared me," she whispered against his chest.

Gustaf set her on her feet, but he didn't let her go. She felt so right in his arms. He tried not to sound harsh. "What you were doing was dangerous. I was afraid you would fall."

She pushed against his chest until there was room between them. "Actually, you caused me to fall. Your shout startled me." At least she didn't sound as though she were accusing him of anything bad.

"Do you often climb like that?" Gustaf stepped away from Olina, giving himself room to breathe.

"Only when I need something from a top shelf." She looked defiantly up at him.

"I can get you anything you want."

"What about when you are not here?" The question came out in a whisper.

"I will bring you a step stool the next time I come." Gustaf looked at the package lying on the floor near the wall. "I brought you something. It's from Sweden."

Olina looked from his face to the box.

"My Bible. Tant Olga has sent my Bible." Olina grabbed the box and clutched it to her heart. "Thank you for bringing it to me."

Gustaf was confused for a moment, then he nodded. He was surprised, but encouraged by Olina's actions. He had been praying for her so long, worrying about her relationship with the Lord. The fact that she had asked her aunt to send her Bible must be a good sign. He decided it would be best to let her open the package alone, so he said a quick good-bye and went to look for Gerda.

❧

Olina knew that Gerda would come back into the house at any moment. She had been out checking the small garden they planted. Olina wanted privacy when she opened the box, so she took it up to her bedroom and closed the door.

Dropping into the rocking chair by the window, she continued to hold the package close as tears streamed down her cheeks. She wasn't sure she was ready to read the words for herself, but she knew she must.

Olina took the package and laid it on the bed. She wondered why Tant Olga had used such a large box to send the Bible. When she opened it, she found out. Letters and two smaller parcels accompanied the book. One letter was in Tant Olga's handwriting, but the writing on the other cried out to her heart. It had been so long since she had seen anything her mother had written.

Grabbing that letter, Olina returned to the rocking chair. Very slowly, she read her mother's words, savoring every one of them.

> *Olina,*
>   *I miss you very much. Olga has let me read your letters. I am so sorry about Lars, but Olina, you are better off without him. If you had married, he might have hurt you later. I am praying for God to heal that pain in your heart.*

Olina paused and gazed at the fluffy clouds floating in the azure sky. She felt disappointment from what had happened with Lars, but the deep hurt was no longer there. When had that happened?

> *Peter has gotten married. I don't think you know the girl. Mary's family had moved here not long before you left for America. They are living with us on the farm. Of course, he is working the farm with your father and John.*
>   *Speaking of your father, I pray daily that he will change his mind about you, but he hasn't yet. Olga said she will pass on my letters to you. And you may write me at Olga's. I visit her as often as I can.*

It was as if Olina could hear her mother's voice as she read.

When she finished the rest of the letter, she placed it lovingly among her handkerchiefs. She knew that she would take it out and read it many times. Tonight, she would write a long letter in return. Hope about her family crept back into Olina's heart.

She went over to the bed and picked up one of the small packages. Turning it over, she saw her mother's handwriting on it. *This belonged to your grandmother. I want you to have it.*

Olina quickly tore the paper from the box. It contained a cameo brooch set in gold. Olina held it in her hand, carefully studying the dainty carved features of a young woman. Her mother's thoughtfulness touched her heart. She would treasure this link with her past.

The other small package was from Tant Olga. The cameo earrings it contained had to be carved by the same craftsman. Olina quickly opened Tant Olga's letter. In it she told that the brooch and earrings had been a set when they were first purchased.

After reading Tant Olga's letter, Olina opened her Bible. The pages fell open to the words she was looking for. She read the verses again and again. The evangelist was right. God did care about what was going on in her life. Olina had never heard anyone explain those particular verses in quite that way, but there was no doubt in her mind what the words were saying.

Father God, forgive me for doubting You. I have been so hurt. Please help me get past that hurt to what You have for me.

It was a simple prayer, but a peace Olina hadn't felt for a long time invaded her heart, returning it to familiar territory. Olina still didn't know what would happen about her father, but her heavenly Father was once again in her life. However, she wondered if He had ever left. Maybe, she had just shut herself off from His presence.

seventeen

Life in the little house bustled. Besides the thriving dressmaking business, Gerda and Olina often had women from town call on them. Sometimes women from the surrounding farms also stopped by on their way to or from town. When that happened, the two young women took time from their busy schedules to share conversations accompanied by refreshments. Olina liked using her grandmother's china teapot to brew the invigorating tea they all enjoyed. Gerda was the one who liked to bake, and she kept a pie, a cake, or dainty pastries on hand for those times of fellowship.

Soon after her Bible had come from Sweden, Gustaf arrived at the house just as Olina was making herself a light lunch. That day, Gerda had gone into town to help Merta make new curtains for her kitchen.

"Are you hungry?" Olina asked when she answered Gustaf's knock. After he nodded, she continued, "I can make us a picnic, and we can eat down by the stream."

Gustaf helped Olina gather together the cold chicken, applesauce, and bread. They put them in a basket, along with a tablecloth to spread on the ground.

After they had finished eating, Olina asked Gustaf, "Do you think that God has specific plans for each person?"

Gustaf took a moment to think about her question. Olina was glad. She wasn't looking for the easy, quick answer.

First, Gustaf asked her a question. "Why are you asking me this?"

Olina watched a cloud that resembled a calf drift across the sky above them. It was hard to put her thoughts into words. "A lot has happened in my life that didn't seem to be good at the time."

Gustaf nodded as if he agreed.

"When we went to the brush arbor meeting, the preacher said that God has plans for us. He read a Scripture that I had never heard before, and he said that it was about the plans God has for us. Do you remember?"

"Vaguely." Gustaf looked as if he were trying to remember.

"That is one reason I asked Tant Olga to send me my Bible. I wanted to read those verses for myself." Olina wasn't sure she should have started this conversation. It was hard to put into words. "I have memorized the words now."

"Tell them to me." Gustaf sounded eager.

" 'For I know the thoughts that I think toward you, saith the Lord, thoughts of peace, and not of evil, to give you an expected end. Then shall ye call upon me, and ye shall go and pray unto me, and I will hearken unto you. And ye shall seek me, and find me, when ye shall search for me with all your heart.' Do you think God was talking about His plans for us like the preacher said?"

Gustaf didn't answer right away. "It could mean that. I know that when I try to make a decision without asking God about it, I often make the wrong decision."

"How do you know whether your decision is right or wrong?"

"Olina, when a decision is the one God would have me make, He gives me peace deep in my heart. It is hard to explain, but that's what it is. Real peace."

When Gustaf left, Olina didn't go back to work. Instead, she took out her Bible and read the verses again. Since her Bible had come from Tant Olga, Olina read it every day. Her relationship with God had grown.

It had been so long since she had read the words of God

that her thirst was almost unquenchable. She looked forward to Sunday, when the Nilsson family attended services at the Lutheran church in Litchfield. Every Sunday, Olina listened eagerly to the words spoken by the pastor. Her whole outlook on life had changed dramatically.

❧

"Olina." Gerda came down the stairs wearing her bonnet and carrying a basket on her arm. "I'm going to the mercantile. We have no more eggs, and we'll soon be out of flour. Do you need anything?"

Olina looked up from the hem she was stitching. "We only have one more needle. It's surprising how many we break."

Gerda laughed. "Maybe we work them too hard. They can't keep up with our speed."

Olina put the dress down on the table and walked over to the sewing machine. "I've been wondering what we would do if the machine needle breaks. Maybe we should have Marja order us a couple of replacement needles, just in case something happens."

"That's a good idea." Gerda took a list from her pocket and wrote on it. "Do you want to come to the store with me?"

Olina picked up the dress again. She sat in the chair by the window and reached into the sewing basket at her feet, taking out the spool of thread. "We promised this dress today, but we don't know when she'll come for it. I think I should work on the hem. I want it finished whenever she comes to pick it up."

After Gerda left, Olina's fingers flew as they made the dainty stitches for which she and Gerda were so famous. Although her hands were busy, her mind kept wandering. It had been three days since Gustaf had come to eat with them. She wondered where he was and why he had stayed away so long. For a moment, she dropped the dress in her lap and looked out the open window. Gustaf's face filled her thoughts as if he were standing there. She could even feel the touch of his hand against her waist. He had been walking beside her on Sunday. When they walked up the steps at church, his hand had touched her back as he guided her. Olina wondered if he even noticed. Probably not. She picked up the dress and continued working on the hem. She should keep her mind on what she was doing and not daydream.

❧

Gustaf drove the wagon into town to pick up supplies for his mother. It was the first day that week he could get away from the farm. One of the hired men was sick, and Gustaf had to do this man's work as well as his own.

He was glad that the horses knew the way to Litchfield. It allowed his thoughts to ramble wherever he wanted. They naturally turned toward Olina. When he was finished in town, he planned to stop by the Nilsson house to check on things, especially Olina. Maybe he would stay for dinner.

Sunday, when they started up the steps at the church, Olina stumbled on the second step, and he touched her to steady her. While it had helped Olina, it did nothing to steady the beat of his heart. Just thinking about it, his hand tingled as it had on Sunday. Whenever there was any kind of physical contact between them, his heart beat double time. Gustaf would hurry gathering the supplies so he could see Olina sooner.

The eastbound train was leaving town when Gustaf pulled up in front of the mercantile. Trains fascinated him. He didn't think he would ever tire of riding them. At the sound of the whistle, Gustaf looked down the street toward the station. A couple standing on the platform beside a pile of luggage looked familiar. At least the man did. If he didn't know better, Gustaf would have been convinced that the man was Lars. But Lars was in Denver. They had received a letter from Lars two weeks ago, and he had not said anything about coming to Minnesota.

The tall man raised a hand and gave a broad wave to Gustaf. Instead of getting out of the wagon, he clucked to the horses, urging them toward the station. Soon he was convinced that the man was Lars. That must be his wife with him. Gustaf had never seen her. She was almost as tall as Lars.

Gustaf had not stopped the wagon before Lars leapt from the platform into the street and shouted, "I thought that was you, Big Brother." Lars stood as if waiting for him to jump from the wagon, but Gustaf just sat where he was.

"Lars, what are you doing here?"

Lars laughed. "You sound as if you aren't glad to see me."

"Of course, I'm glad to see you. I'm a little. . .surprised."

"That's what we wanted to do. Surprise everyone."

Gustaf frowned. "Surprises aren't always a good thing. There are some people who might be uncomfortable by your surprise."

"Who would that be?"

Gustaf jumped down from the wagon seat and spoke quietly to Lars. "Do you know that Olina is still here?"

"Yes." Lars looked a little uncomfortable. "I need to talk to Olina face-to-face."

"That might not be a good idea." Gustaf tried not to sound too angry, but when he thought about what Lars had done to Olina, the anger came anyway.

Lars spoke to Gustaf, man to man. "It's something I have to do. I'm not proud of what I did to Olina. I need to make amends for it."

"Lars, is everything all right?" The feminine voice called from the station platform.

Lars gestured toward the woman standing on the platform, and Gustaf looked up at her.

The woman smiled.

"Come meet my wife." Lars took Gustaf by the arm and

pulled him along up the steps. "Janice, this is my oldest brother."

She placed her gloved hand into Gustaf's. "I think I would have known you anywhere, Gustaf. Lars has told me so much about you." Her voice had a lyrical quality to it.

Gustaf hadn't known what to expect in his sister-in-law. She was tall and willowy. Her friendly face was surrounded by abundant black hair, styled in the current pompadour fashion. Her eyes were her most arresting feature. They were green, sparkling with life. For a moment Gustaf questioned his brother's sanity. Janice was beautiful, but she didn't come close to Olina in any area that he could see.

Gustaf gave Lars and Janice a ride to the hotel. They had decided to stay there for the first few nights of their visit. They thought it would make everything less awkward. It was a good thing that Gustaf hadn't yet bought the supplies. There wouldn't have been room in the wagon for all of their luggage and everything he came to pick up.

When they came back out of the hotel after taking the luggage up to their room, Gerda was walking down the sidewalk near the mercantile. She saw Lars before he saw her, and she came hurrying across the street, calling out to them.

Gustaf suggested that Gerda, Lars, and Janice go into the hotel. He told them he would pick up Olina and bring her back so they could have lunch together. When Gerda looked concerned, he told her that he would prepare Olina for the confrontation.

As Gustaf drove the wagon toward his house, he started praying for Olina. He wanted to warn her about Lars, and he wanted to be with her when she learned that he was in Litchfield. If need be, Gustaf was prepared to stay at the house with Olina until she didn't need him anymore. He hoped that Lars and Janice's presence wouldn't set Olina back in her walk with the Lord. Most of all, Gustaf didn't want Olina hurt again.

&

Olina was finishing the last stitch in the hem of the ruffled skirt when she noticed Gustaf's wagon coming from Litchfield. She hadn't seen him go by on the way to town. It was hard to miss him now. He was driving fast. That was unusual for Gustaf. He was always careful with the horses. Olina stood up and stretched. Then she took the dress to the table to fold it. She was glad that she could see outside from every spot in the room. With one eye on what she was doing, she kept part of her attention on the wagon that was approaching the house.

When Gustaf stopped the wagon in front, Olina went to the door. Maybe he was coming to eat lunch with them. It was too bad that they hadn't cooked anything today. Olina was planning to make a sandwich with some of the tomatoes out of the garden and the piece of ham left from breakfast. That would barely feed her. It wouldn't be enough for a hardworking man like Gustaf.

Olina opened the door just as Gustaf stepped onto the porch. "Hello. Have you come for—?" The look on Gustaf's face stopped the question in midsentence. She rushed through the door. "Oh, Gustaf, what's the matter?" Without thinking, she reached up and cupped her hand on his cheek.

Gustaf placed his calloused fingers on top of hers as if to hold them in place. "Olina, I must talk to you."

"You're scaring me. Whatever has happened to cause you this distress?" Olina couldn't pull her gaze from his.

He looked as if he were worried about her. Why would he be worried about her? Had he heard something in town? She glanced down at his other hand. It didn't hold any mail, so it couldn't be anything bad about her family.

Gustaf pulled her hand from his face and held it in both his hands. "Let's sit here."

Olina and Gerda loved sitting on the porch in the cool of the evening, so Gustaf and August had built a wooden swing for them. Gustaf guided her toward the swing. When they were seated, he leaned his forearms on his knees and clasped his hands.

"I've come to tell you something."

Olina was exasperated. "So tell me. Don't keep me wondering any longer."

Gustaf leaned back and placed his arm along the back of the swing. "Someone came to Litchfield on the train that just went through."

"So?" Olina knew that people often came to Litchfield on the train. She looked up into his troubled eyes and waited.

"It was Lars and his wife." The statement hung in the air between them while Gustaf seemed to be studying every expression on Olina's face. What was he looking for?

"Lars. . .and his wife?" Olina was puzzled.

"Yes." Gustaf took one of her hands in his.

"I didn't know that he was coming home."

"No one did." He rubbed the back of her hand with his thumb while he continued to study her. "It's a surprise visit."

Olina waited for the hurt to settle in her chest, but all she felt was surprised. *Oh, Father, did You take that hurt away, too? Will I be able to forgive Lars as You have forgiven me?* "Where are they?"

Gustaf must have been holding his breath because he had to let it out to answer her. "I left them at the hotel with Gerda. Do you feel like going into town to see them?"

Olina stood up and walked to the porch railing. She leaned against it, looking toward town as if she could see into the hotel. Then she turned back to Gustaf. "It was inevitable that this would happen. We might as well get it over with, but I need to freshen up a bit."

Gustaf's smile went right to Olina's heart. "I'll be here when you are ready."

"I'll hurry."

Gerda, Lars, and his wife were sitting in the lobby visiting when Gustaf and Olina arrived. Lars stood as if he had been watching the door for them. Standing across the room from her was the man she had planned to marry. For a moment, all the pain lanced through Olina's heart. How was she going to get through the next few minutes? She just had to. She closed her eyes and took a deep breath. Did she need to stop all feeling again as she had before? Would it help?

Lars introduced Olina to Janice. *What does he see in her that he didn't see in me?* Olina recognized the wariness in Janice's expression. It wasn't her fault, was it? Lars hadn't been a real man. He hadn't taken responsibility for his actions, and two women were paying a price for that irresponsibility. When Lars met Janice, did he even tell her about Olina?

After introducing Olina to Janice, Lars asked Olina if she would take a walk with him. She looked at Janice, who nodded.

They walked around the hotel and out across a field toward a small grove of trees. When they reached the shade, Lars stopped Olina with a gentle touch on her arm. She turned toward him.

"Olina, we came to visit with our family, but you're the main reason I've come."

She looked up at him and waited. It was a minute or two before he continued. During that time, he studied her as if he were looking for something specific.

"I know that I did you a grave injustice." Lars seemed ill at ease. He shifted his weight from one foot to the other. "I was blind to my faults. And I was impulsive."

Olina nodded. She agreed wholeheartedly.

"I should have met you in New York City. I apologize for that. Can you forgive me?"

Olina gazed up at a cloud that was drifting by. It looked like a little lamb, gamboling in the pasture around his mother. The lamb reminded her of Jesus, who died to bring her forgiveness.

Looking back at Lars, she whispered, "Yes, I will work on forgiving you." She paused, then continued. "Why did you go to Denver in the first place, Lars?" She had to know.

Once again, Lars shuffled his feet in the grass. "I thought we could start our new life together in Denver. I was offered a better paying job, and I planned to get us a home, then come back here before you arrived. I planned for us to be married here and then go to our new home." He looked everywhere but at her, taking a long time before he blurted, "I thought I loved you, Olina, but I didn't know what love really was until I met Janice. "

Olina waited for the pain to lance though her midsection. She felt disappointment, but not the agony she expected. "And what is love. . .really?"

"It's not just that she's beautiful. You're beautiful, too. Janice and I were made for each other. She has strengths where I have weaknesses, and I have strengths in the areas where she is weak. I know God created someone for you, just as he created Janice and me to be together."

When Lars said that, Olina looked across the field toward town, and her thoughts drifted to Gustaf. Could he be the one?

"I have great fondness for you." Lars's voice sounded stronger, more sure. "You will always have a special place in my heart."

Olina glanced back at him. "Maybe that's not good."

"Janice knows all about you. . .us. . .what we were to each other. At least now she knows. I was not man enough to tell her about you until after we were engaged." Lars rubbed the back of his neck. "We were not meant for each other, you and I. We just thought we were. I know it'll be hard for you to forgive me for all of this, but that's what I came here for. To apologize to you face-to-face. I pray that someday we can be friends."

Olina glanced at the grass, then across the field to some cows that were grazing in the adjoining pasture. "I'll not deny that you hurt me very much. I don't know when I've ever been so hurt." She looked down at her skirt that the gentle wind was swirling around her ankles. "I'm trying to forgive you. In time, maybe we'll be comfortable around each other." She gazed up at Lars. "We should go back. I don't want the others to be worried about us."

Lars took her arm and guided her back to the front of the hotel.

On the way across the field, Olina thought about all she had gone through. Had God allowed those things to happen because He had created someone for her, someone besides Lars? Was he here in Litchfield, Minnesota, right now?

What about Janice? She had been caught in the middle of the dilemma Lars had caused by his irresponsible actions.

Just as she stepped up on the wooden sidewalk, Olina said, "I'm glad you've come. I do want to get to know your wife."

⁂

When Gustaf drove Olina home, Gerda stayed in town with Lars and Janice. He was glad, because he wanted to talk to Olina alone.

After stopping the horses by the front gate, Gustaf turned to Olina. "Are you all right?"

Olina looked up at Gustaf. "You mean about Lars and Janice?"

"That. . .and about Lars being here. . .and about Lars and you."

Olina blinked as if her eyes were watering. "There is no 'Lars and me.'"

Gustaf reached over and took both her hands in his. "I know that, but how are you handling everything?"

When Olina looked down at their clasped hands, so did Gustaf. Hers looked so small and smooth, engulfed in his large, calloused ones. He would gladly take all the pain out of her life, but he knew he couldn't.

Olina looked back up at him. "I want to forgive Lars, but it is so hard, for sure. How can I completely forgive him? The hurt goes deep."

Gustaf didn't know if he had an answer for her, so he got out of the wagon, then helped Olina down. They walked to the front door in silence.

"Let's look in the Bible, Olina." Gustaf opened the door and waited for her to enter.

Olina went into the parlor and picked her Bible up from the table where she had put it when she finished reading it last night. "What do you want to show me?"

Gustaf sat on the sofa, and Olina sat beside him. Gustaf searched for a verse. "In Matthew, chapter six, it says, 'And forgive us our debts, as we forgive our debtors.'"

Olina nodded. "I remember reading that. It's where Jesus teaches His disciples how to pray, isn't it?"

"Yes. But it was more than that." Gustaf cleared his throat. He didn't want to hurt Olina, but he wanted her to understand what he was talking about. "I believe it means that if we don't forgive others, then the Lord won't forgive us."

"That's a hard word, Gustaf."

"I know, but when you forgive others, it allows your forgiveness from God to flow freely. Does that make any sense?"

Olina nodded. "I see what you mean. And I think I agree, but it's not easy sometimes."

Gustaf stood and walked to the front window. "God didn't say that everything would be easy, but it would be worth it. I had a hard time forgiving Lars for what he did. God used this verse to teach me that I had to. It took me awhile, and I thought I had totally forgiven him."

Gustaf rubbed the back of his neck with one hand. "Then today when I saw him on that platform. . .and knew that his coming could cause you pain, my anger came back. While I was coming for you, God reminded me that I had forgiven Lars. If you are never able to forgive Lars, there'll be a root of bitterness growing inside your heart. Soon it will consume you." He turned back toward Olina. "You don't want that, do you?"

Olina shook her head. "No, I don't. Would you pray for me?"

"We can do that right now." Gustaf sat back down beside Olina. "Father God, please help Olina turn loose of the bitterness and unforgiveness she has in her heart. Give her Your strength. Let Your love for Lars flow through her heart and take its place. We pray this in Jesus' name. Amen."

eighteen

Lars and Janice stayed at Litchfield for a month. Because Lars decided to help with the harvesting at the farm, after a few days, he and Janice moved into the house with his parents. Gerda and Olina became friends with Janice. Often when the men were working at the farm, Janice spent the day at Gerda and Olina's home, even helping them with handwork or cooking lunch for them while they finished a garment. In the evenings, Gerda, Olina, and August ate dinner at the farm. Everyone wanted to make the most of the time Lars and Janice were there.

One Friday night in September, all the family was gathered around the table enjoying another one of Mrs. Nilsson's wonderful meals. Gerda noticed that Gustaf seemed preoccupied. She wondered what was bothering him, but she didn't have long to worry.

"A few of the shingles on my house look as if they're damaged." Gustaf took another bite of the chicken and dumplings. Olina knew it was one of his favorite foods. He looked thoughtful while he chewed. "Since we don't have any other fields ready for harvest right now, I think I'll go over and fix the roof tomorrow." He looked around the table at his brothers. "Do you want to help me?"

Lars put down his fork and frowned. "I would like to, but Janice promised her aunt and uncle that we would spend the day with them."

Janice smiled at her husband. "It would be all right if you want to help your brother. I can go without you."

"No," Gustaf said. "You haven't spent much of your time here with the Braxtons. It's only right that you both go tomorrow."

"I can help you." August reached for another hot roll. "I haven't had a day off, except Sunday, for a long time. We aren't very busy right now."

Gustaf smiled. "Then it's settled. I'll feel better about the girls spending the winter in the house if I know the roof is safe."

The next morning, Gustaf and August arrived in time for breakfast. Gerda had told Olina that they would, so the young women had cooked extra bacon and biscuits. Gerda started the scrambled eggs while the men washed up for the meal.

Breakfast was fun, with light banter going around the room and keeping everyone laughing between bites. Olina looked at Gustaf. She liked having him sitting across the table from her. It was familiar and something she would like to continue for her whole life. Where had that thought come from? She sat stunned, wondering what it meant.

August pushed his chair back from the table. "We'd better get started if we want to finish today."

"Okay, Brother." Gustaf clapped him on the back before he went out the door toward the wagon.

Olina sat for a minute more, still stunned by the direction of her thoughts. Gerda quickly cleaned off the table. Olina jumped up and started washing the dishes while Gerda dried them and put them away.

"I'm going to the mercantile this morning." Gerda hung the tea towel on a hook near the sink. "Do you want to go with me?"

"Not today," Olina said. "Last week I bought a piece of wool to make myself a suit. I haven't even had time to cut it out. I want to get it made before the weather gets any colder."

"Do you want me to get anything for you while I'm there?"

Olina followed Gerda out of the kitchen. "Would you check and see if they have any cotton sateen? I want to make a new waist to go with the suit."

Gerda stopped and put on her bonnet and shawl. "What color?"

"The wool is navy. Maybe a light blue, pink, or even white would go with it."

Olina went into the sewing room and pulled the fabric from the shelf. She planned to make a skirt that wasn't as full as she wore in the summer. She liked a little flare, but if it wasn't too full, the skirt would be warmer. The wind was bad about blowing full skirts around, and the wind already had a bite to it. Olina wanted to make a fitted jacket with fitted sleeves. That style was also warmer than looser styles. If she had enough fabric, Olina was going to add a peplum to the bottom of the jacket. Maybe she would scallop it to give it more interest. She could even add scallops to the opening of the jacket, with a buttonhole in each scallop. The more she envisioned the new creation, the more excited she became. Spreading the fabric on the table, Olina went to work cutting out the suit.

Gustaf and August quickly gathered the needed tools and wooden shingles from the wagon. While Gustaf carried them to the side of the house, August hefted the ladder on his broad shoulders.

It took several trips up and down the ladder before the men had moved all they needed to work with onto the roof. Soon they were pulling away rotted shingles and nailing new ones into place. While they worked, the brothers talked and laughed. They had always gotten along, and they worked well together.

It took them most of the morning to finish the back of the

roof. Then they moved across to the front. Gustaf placed his tools and nails within easy reach, but they had used most of the shingles they brought up earlier.

"I need more shingles." Gustaf stood and stretched his muscles. He wasn't used to all this hammering and crawling on his knees. He rotated his right shoulder while holding it with his left hand. "How about you?"

"Sure." August laid his hammer down and pulled a bandanna from his back pocket to wipe the sweat from his forehead. "I've used most of mine."

"I'll go down and get some more." Gustaf started over the top of the roof, but one of the shingles he stepped on broke, and he lost his balance. Standing on a slope wasn't easy, and he couldn't regain his balance. He tried to clutch at anything that would stop him as he tumbled down the few feet to the edge of the roof, then he plunged through the air. A primitive cry forced its way from his throat before he hit the ground two stories below. Then everything went black.

❧

At first, the sound of the pounding had bothered Olina, but soon the rhythm was soothing. One of the men hit a nail, followed immediately by the other man's pound. It didn't take Olina long before she knew which pound was which. Although Gustaf hit the nails with power, because of his work at the blacksmith's, August's pounds were harder. *Ba Boom. Ba Boom.* The rhythm continued. It was a comforting sound, much like her mother's heartbeat when she had held Olina close as a child. The sounds would stop as the men moved to another spot, only to resume again.

Olina tried to keep her thoughts from wandering to Gustaf. She didn't want to make any mistakes as she cut out the suit. If she was careful, she could make the outfit the way she wanted and still have enough fabric left to make a matching reticule. She could line the purse with the fabric from the blouse she would make to go with the suit.

There was never a minute when Olina wasn't aware that Gustaf was on the roof above her. She knew when the men moved to the area above the sewing room, even though a bedroom was between the roof and the room where she worked. Once again the pounding stopped. She imagined the men taking a break.

"Aaiiee!"

The primitive scream was followed by a dull thump right outside the sewing room. For a moment Olina was paralyzed. Then she rushed to the window and raised it. What she saw caused her to catch her breath. Gustaf lay motionless on the ground.

Olina quickly leaned out and looked toward the eaves. August leaned over, gazing at his brother with anguish covering his face.

"What happened?" Olina's question sounded shrill even to her own ears.

August shook his head. "I don't know for sure. He was going for more shingles. . .and then he was—" August couldn't continue.

"Come down right now." Olina turned and hurried toward the front door.

She ran around to the side of the house and crumpled beside the still unmoving body. She doubled over and sobs tore from deep within her.

When August came around the house, he knelt on the other side of his brother. Tears were making their way down his cheeks. "He's not dead, Olina."

Olina looked up.

"See. He's breathing." August pointed to Gustaf's chest, which was moving with each breath.

"Should we move him into the house?" Olina looked toward the structure.

"That might not be a good idea." August stood. "What if something is broken? We could injure him more. . . . I'm going for the doctor."

Olina scrambled to her feet. "What can I do?"

"Stay with him." August strode across the yard toward his horse, but he swerved to head to the wagon, then stopped and turned to look back at Olina and Gustaf. "Maybe you should cover him with something warm."

Olina ran into the house and up the stairs to her bedroom. She jerked the quilt from her bed and grabbed her pillow. After hurrying down the stairs and around the house, she gently cradled Gustaf's head in her arms while she pushed the pillow under it. Then she covered him with the quilt and pushed it in close to his body all around. It became soiled, but she didn't care. Nothing was important except Gustaf.

As Olina gazed at his face, her heart felt as if it had burst open, and all the love that had been building for Gustaf poured forth. She loved him with her whole heart. Olina didn't know when this had happened, but she really loved him. More than she had ever loved Lars. More than she had realized was even possible. That love hurt because Gustaf was injured.

"Father God," Olina wailed. "Please help Gustaf." She pulled the bottom of her skirt up and wiped the tears from her face, but they continued to pour from her eyes. "I love him, Father God. Please don't take him away from me just when I've discovered that I love him."

Olina reached and pushed his hair from his forehead. Then her hand continued around his cheek and came to rest on his strong neck. Olina could feel the blood pulsing through the vein there. Surely he wouldn't die while his pulse was so strong.

"Please, God, I beg You. Let him not be badly hurt. I don't care if he'll never be mine. I love him enough to want the best for him. Let him be okay. I want to see him every day." The last sentence ended on a sob.

The first thing Gustaf became aware of was the cold hard ground beneath him. He fought to open his eyes but was unable to keep from drifting back into the blackness.

The next time he fought his way up out of the dark, he noticed that he felt warmer. Something soft was under his head, something warm had settled over him, and someone was tucking it in around his body. It felt good. He tried to open his eyes, but he still couldn't. Then he heard the voice.

Olina, sweet Olina, was praying. For him. She said that she loved him. He wanted to try to open his eyes again, but decided against it. He would wait to hear what else she had to say. When her hand touched his head, he almost flinched because it surprised him so much. As it continued down his face, he reveled in the feel of her soft flesh against his. He would remember the way it felt as long as he lived. When her hand rested on his neck, Gustaf knew she could feel his pulse. His heartbeat had quickened so much at her touch. He couldn't wait any longer. He had to look at her.

Olina was studying Gustaf's face when his eyes fluttered open. She tried to pull back, but one of his arms snaked out from under the quilt and his hand grabbed hers. When she relaxed, his touch became gentle. She was unable to tear her gaze from his eyes. They seemed to hold her captive, and she read an answering love in them. Could it be that he loved her as she loved him?

Before long, August, Gerda, and the doctor hurried around the side of the house.

"I see that he has recovered consciousness." The doctor's voice boomed.

Startled, Olina turned and tried to get up, but Gustaf didn't let her hand go, so she sank back onto the ground beside him.

The doctor set his black bag on the ground beside Gustaf and took out his stethoscope. He listened to Gustaf's breathing through his chest and took his pulse.

"Do you have any pain, Son?" the fatherly man asked.

Gustaf looked toward the man. "Yes. I kind of hurt all over."

"Is there any place that it is localized?" The doctor started probing his body, searching for broken bones.

"I don't think so, Sir." Gustaf moved first one arm and then the other. "Maybe I'm just sore. I know I had the breath knocked out of me."

"He was knocked unconscious for several minutes," Olina informed the doctor.

"Well, can you move everything?" The doctor watched as Gustaf moved his arms, his legs, and his head. "Does anything hurt worse when you move it?"

"Not that I can tell." Gustaf tried to sit up, and the doctor gave him a hand.

"Are you dizzy?" The doctor looked at Gustaf's pupils.

"No, Sir. Is it all right if I stand up?"

The doctor helped him to his feet. Then he looked at the ground where Gustaf had been lying. "If you were going to fall off a house, it's a good thing you picked this place to land."

Gustaf looked down, too.

"See? There's enough grass to cushion your fall, and there are no rocks to harm you." The doctor touched his shoulder. "Come inside, Son. I would like to do a thorough examination, to be on the safe side."

Olina followed the men into the house. She was glad that nothing seemed to be seriously injured.

nineteen

After the doctor finished the examination, he and Gustaf came back downstairs. Olina looked up expectantly, waiting for the doctor's verdict.

"Well, young man, you are lucky." The doctor nodded his head as he spoke.

"I believe that God protected me," Gustaf told him. "Maybe my guardian angel caught me and lowered me to the ground."

The doctor glanced at the others before he answered. "If that's what you want to think." He put his bag down on a chair and dug through it. After pulling out a package, he placed it in Gustaf's hand. "This is Epsom salt. Go home. Take a hot bath and put some of this salt in your bath water. It should take out the soreness. Didn't I hear that your folks have one of those newfangled water heaters at your house?"

"Yes." Gustaf took the proffered remedy. "I'm glad we do. It'll come in handy today."

After the doctor drove off in his buggy, August looked at Gustaf. "You take my horse and ride home. I'll bring your wagon later."

"Why?" Gustaf looked as if he was going to refuse. "What are you going to do?"

August gestured toward the roof. "Go up there and finish what we started."

Gustaf shook his head. "I'll do it another day."

"No need for that. It won't take me long." August glanced from Gustaf to Gerda and Olina. "When I'm finished, I'll bring the girls home for dinner. By that time, you might be feeling better."

August accompanied Gustaf to the horse. It looked to Olina, who was watching from the window, as though Gustaf was arguing about it, but August must have won, because Gustaf mounted the horse. August loaded more shingles onto his shoulder before he started back up the ladder. While he finished the roof that afternoon, Olina wished for Gustaf's part in the hammering rhythm.

When August, Gerda, and Olina arrived at the Nilsson farm for dinner, Olina was glad to see Gustaf sitting in the parlor. She stopped in the doorway and watched him. He was engrossed in reading his Bible. It allowed her a few undisturbed moments to study him. As if someone had told him that she was there, Gustaf glanced up. He smiled, then rose slowly.

"Come in, Olina," he said, his voice husky with emotion.

Olina caught her breath. "P–perhaps I should see if your mother needs any help with dinner." She turned to go.

"Come in, Olina. We are alone, and we need to talk."

Olina's right hand fluttered to her throat. "Right now?" Her question sounded breathless, even to her own ears.

Gustaf looked around. "Now would be a good time."

Olina took one step into the room. It seemed to be filled with the presence of Gustaf, leaving little space for her. She took a hesitant breath. There wasn't even enough air for both of them to breathe comfortably.

Gustaf walked toward her. "Are you suddenly afraid of me, Olina?"

She shook her head in denial. Gustaf stopped right in front of her, but he didn't reach out to her. Olina didn't know what to say to him. All afternoon she had wondered if he had heard any of the words of her prayer. He was standing so close that the heat of his body reached out and enveloped her.

"You weren't afraid of me this morning, dear Olina." The soft words were for her ears alone, and the endearment touched her heart.

Olina dropped her gaze to his muscled chest, but that didn't help her breathe any easier. "Why do you say that, Gustaf?"

A gentle chuckle rumbled from him, causing his chest to rise and fall. "Do you love me, Olina?"

Her wary gaze flew to his. Once again, she saw the loving expression from that morning. "Why do you ask?"

Gustaf reached out and pulled her into his arms. With her nestled against his chest, he rested his chin on top of her head. Olina was glad she had worn her hair in a simple chignon at the nape of her neck. Nothing was in the way of his chin. Its touch felt like a caress. She closed her eyes and sighed.

"I heard a voice calling me out of the darkness this morning."

Olina's eyes flew open. That startling statement answered the questions she had wrestled with all day. He had heard her. But how much had he heard?

As if she had spoken the question aloud, Gustaf answered. "I heard you praying for God to heal me. You told Him that you love me." He leaned back a little and placed one finger under her chin, raising it until her gaze met his. "You wouldn't lie to God, would you? Do you love me?"

A large lump in her throat kept Olina from voicing her answer, so she nodded.

"Enough to marry me, Olina?"

Olina's heart almost burst with happiness.

Before she could answer, Gerda came from the kitchen. "Olina, Gustaf—" She stopped short. "I'm not interrupting anything, am I?"

"Yes."

"No."

Gustaf and Olina answered at the same time. Then they

burst out laughing, but Gustaf didn't release Olina from the shelter of his arms.

"Is there something you would like to tell me?" Gerda looked from one to the other.

"Yes."

"No."

Once again, they answered in unison.

Now Gerda was laughing with them. "Well, Gustaf keeps telling me 'yes,' and Olina keeps telling me 'no.' Which is it?"

Olina could feel a blush creep up over her neck and face while Gustaf answered. "Yes, we'll have something to tell you but not right now. You'll know what's going on soon enough."

Gerda rolled her eyes and went back into the kitchen. "Mother, is it time to ring the dinner bell?" Gustaf and Olina could hear her elevated tone. "Father and August are in the barn, but Gustaf and Olina are in the parlor."

The next thing Olina heard was the dinner bell. Although it was the most wonderful place she had ever been, Olina pulled herself from Gustaf's embrace and put her hands on her cheeks to try to cool them.

"That won't take away your becoming blush." Gustaf touched his forefinger to the tip of her nose, then turned toward the kitchen, but he whispered into her ear as he went by. "I will get an answer to my question before the evening is over."

The meal Mrs. Nilsson had prepared was a veritable feast. A succulent ham was accompanied by roasted potatoes, green beans, and the last tomatoes from the garden. Fresh churned butter melted into the hot rolls. Some of the butter dripped down Olina's chin when she took her first bite. She patted her chin with her napkin and glanced toward Gustaf once again. His face held a secret smile that touched her heart.

Although everything tasted wonderful, Olina couldn't eat more than a few bites. Her stomach did flip-flops every time she glanced up at Gustaf to find his intent gaze trained on her face. Soon she was moving the food around her plate instead of putting it in her mouth. Gustaf wanted to marry her.

Father God, is this Your plan for me? When Olina asked the question in her heart, she felt a peace there, but the turmoil in the rest of her body continued. What was the matter with her? Was this jumpy feeling in the pit of her stomach a prelude to some illness?

Olina was drawing circles in the gravy on her plate with her fork when she felt Gerda's foot nudge hers. She looked up to find every eye in the room trained on her. The blush that had died down once more stained her cheeks.

"I asked you, Dear, if you were feeling all right." Mrs. Nilsson looked concerned. "You've hardly eaten any of your dinner. I hope you're not getting sick."

"No." Olina smiled at her hostess. "I guess I have had too much excitement for one day." Olina didn't look directly at Gustaf, but out of the corner of her eye, she could see his smile widen.

"Yes, well." Mr. Nilsson harrumphed to clear his throat. "I wanted to tell you girls how proud I am of you."

Everyone's attention turned toward the head of the table.

"Why is that, Father?" Gerda asked.

"I can't help but worry about you." He looked toward Gustaf. "Of course your brother keeps me informed about how you're doing, but I wondered if you needed any monetary help." Olina started to comment, but before she could, Mr. Nilsson continued. "When I was at the bank this afternoon, I asked Mr. Finley if I needed to put some money into your account. He informed me that you each had a very healthy account indeed."

"It helps that Gustaf isn't charging us any rent." Gerda smiled at her brother.

He laughed in return. "No rent, except several hot meals each week."

"Which you don't need, since your mother feeds you quite well." Olina looked him full in the face for the first time during the meal.

His gaze was so intent that she couldn't look away. "It's a good time to make sure you are safe and don't need anything."

Everything around them seemed to fade away, leaving only Gustaf and Olina, with an invisible, mysterious connection— even across the table.

Finally, Mrs. Nilsson arose from her chair and began cleaning off the table. Gerda quickly assisted her. When Olina also started to help, Gustaf asked her if she would take a walk with him.

"I need to keep the stiffness worked out of my body." His eyes compelled her more than his words. "Please accompany me."

They strolled halfway down the long drive in companionable silence before Gustaf brought up the subject that was on both of their minds.

"Are you ready to give me your answer, Olina?"

At his words, Olina stopped and turned toward him. Before she could answer, he laughed. Gustaf took her hands in both of his. "Are you going to make me kneel and ask you again? It might be hard for me to get up afterward."

The picture of her trying to pull the tall, strong man up caused Olina to laugh, too. "Yes. I love you enough to marry you."

After a moment, Gustaf asked, "Do I hear a 'but' at the end of your sentence?"

"I want to marry you, but I need to make things right with Fader. When you shared that Scripture with me about forgiving as God would forgive, it made me realize that I need to forgive Fader as much as I must forgive Lars. I've finally come to the point where I have forgiven him in my heart. I was planning to write a letter to him asking his forgiveness for going against his wishes. Would you wait for the wedding until I can write him? I've come so far since I started listening to the Lord again, but I still feel I can't move on with my life without taking care of this matter."

Gustaf pulled her into his embrace again. Cradling her against his strong chest, he whispered, "You are so special. I'll wait as long as you need me to. I do believe that God intends for us to be together."

Olina nodded against his chest. "I do, too."

"It'll give me time to court you properly."

❧

Gustaf liked the feel of Olina in his arms. As they stood with her soft, warm body pressed against his leanness, he thought of her strawberry-colored mouth. He wondered how it would feel to press his lips to hers and savor the sweetness that was the essence of Olina. She must have sensed some of what he felt, because she raised her face from against his chest and looked up into his face.

Gustaf's gaze dropped to her trembling lips. He lowered his head slightly, then hesitated, to give her time to pull away. Olina's adoring gaze never wavered, so he continued his descent.

Gustaf had never kissed a woman. He had never felt this burning desire to taste a woman's lips before. The first touch was tentative and gentle. Gustaf savored Olina's sweetness, then settled his lips more firmly against hers.

For a moment, or an eon of time, he reveled in the feel of Olina. All too soon, Gustaf broke the earth-shattering kiss. He once again cradled her head against his chest. He felt sure she heard his heartbeat thunder against her ear. How easily he could have lost himself in their togetherness. But

Gustaf knew that if they were going to wait awhile before marrying, he needed to protect Olina from his strong human urges. *Father, help me be the man she needs.*

When Gustaf and Olina gazed into each other's eyes, she felt it to her very foundation. She had never realized how strong the connection between two people in love could be. Then Gustaf's gaze dropped to her lips. She could feel the intensity of his attention. It caused her to lick her lips because they felt dry.

As Gustaf's head lowered toward hers, Olina held her breath. She knew that he was going to kiss her. For an instant, he hesitated. She recognized that he was giving her a chance to step back. But Olina didn't want to. She welcomed his kiss with all the love she felt for him.

Gustaf was so strong. His muscles were rock hard, but his lips were soft. His gentleness reached toward her. And then the kiss deepened. Everything faded from Olina's awareness except Gustaf. Wrapped in his love, she felt protected. Her arms crept around his waist.

Too soon, Gustaf broke the kiss, but he pulled her against his chest. . .and his beating heart. She could tell by the rhythm of the heartbeats that he was as affected by their kiss as she was.

Gustaf turned toward the house and started walking with one arm around Olina, holding her securely by his side. "Now we must tell my family, but I don't think they'll be surprised."

twenty

That night, Olina wrote a long letter to her mother, explaining all that had happened. She included another to her father, asking for his forgiveness. After writing a note to Tant Olga, she enclosed all the missives in one envelope addressed to her great-aunt. Olina sealed the envelope, then placed both hands on the thick bundle and prayed over it, asking God to direct every word to the hearts of those receiving them. When she finished this task, her heart felt lighter.

During the rest of the autumn, Olina and Gerda were busy with their dressmaking. News of their expertise spread, and some women even came from other towns to order dresses from them.

Olina no longer felt the need to protect her financial security as she had, so she and Gerda purchased things to make their cottage more homey. They chose fabric to make all new curtains and even bought a few small pieces of furniture. Tables and lamps added warmth to the living room. Scraps of fabric were fashioned into pillows that made the sofa more inviting,

Gustaf kept his promise to court Olina. He escorted her to every party and social that was held in Litchfield or at any of the surrounding farms. It wasn't long until everyone knew that the two planned to marry. They received many congratulations, even from Anna Jenson, who was being courted by one of the other young farmers in the area.

Olina hoped that she would hear from her father in a month or two after she sent the letter. By mid-November, she went every day to the post office, which was located in the mercantile, to check for a letter. Every day that didn't bring an answer caused a heaviness in her heart. She feared that her father was still angry with her. How would she ever have total peace if he continued to shut her out?

Thanksgiving was fast approaching. Olina had never experienced this holiday, since it was distinctly American. She was excited while the family began preparations. In addition to their grain crops, the Nilssons raised cattle. However, for Thanksgiving, August went hunting for venison. When he brought in a large buck three days before the holiday, the whole family worked on preparing the meat. The two hindquarters were smoked, much like the hams of a pig. The forelegs were roasted, and the rest of the meat was made into sausage, then smoked.

On Thanksgiving Day, their church hosted a community-wide celebration. A morning service allowed everyone to express thanks to God for their blessings that year. Olina thanked God for bringing her to America and giving her Gustaf to love, but a small part of her heart ached for the loss of her Swedish family. She prayed silently for God to intervene there, too.

The pews were moved into a storeroom, and tables and benches were brought in for the dinner. Everyone had prepared their best.

The Nilssons shared the roasted forelegs and one hindquarter of their deer. Others brought ham, pork chops, beef roasts, or chickens. Olina imagined that the tables groaned under the weight of all the food. Vegetable dishes, pies, cakes, pastries, hot breads, fresh churned butter. The aromas started her mouth watering long before the meal began.

Soon after Thanksgiving, everyone was preparing for Christmas. Olina and Gerda worked together to make all the members of Gerda's family some new garment. While they were visiting at the farm, Gerda sneaked around and measured her father's and Gustaf's shirts. The young women offered to do August's laundry with theirs, so they were able to measure his shirt, too.

Pooling the amount of money they could afford to spend, they bought the best fabric available in Litchfield. They made each man a new dress shirt. Mrs. Nilsson would receive a wool suit, complete with a silk waist to wear with it.

One week before Christmas, Olina went to town to pick out lace for the dress she was secretly creating for Gerda. When she finished making all her purchases, she went to the corner where the post office was located. Once again, she was disappointed to find no letter from Sweden waiting for her. With her head down against the cold wind, she started the walk toward the cottage. She didn't notice the vehicle driving by until she heard her name called.

Olina almost dropped her package. The voice calling her sounded so much like her mother's voice that tears pooled in her eyes. When she looked up, she saw August driving a buggy from the livery. The tears blurred her vision so that she didn't recognize the woman sitting on the other side of him.

"Olina." August stopped right beside her. "Look who has come to visit you."

He jumped from the buggy and turned back to help the woman to the sidewalk. Olina reached into her reticule and withdrew a handkerchief to wipe her eyes. When she looked up, she saw that her ears had not deceived her.

"Mor!" Olina dropped the package and threw her arms around the woman her heart had missed all these months. With tears streaming down her face, Olina hugged her mother as if she would never let go.

"Darling, don't cry." Brigitta Sandstrom said in Swedish, as she pulled back from the embrace to look at her daughter's face. "I only wanted to make you happy."

Olina was used to conversing in English, but she easily went back into her native tongue. "Oh, you have. These are happy tears." Then Olina looked around. "Where is Fader?"

Brigitta and August looked at each other. August picked the package up from the wooden sidewalk. "Olina, I'll take you and your mother to your house. We'll be there in a few minutes and then you can talk all you want."

"Could Fader not come?"

"Come, Dear." Brigitta took Olina by the arm. "This wind is so cold. Let's get in out of it, and I'll tell you all about it."

Olina was so pleased to be with Mor that she climbed into the buggy for the ride. Thankfully, it only took a few minutes.

Once they arrived at the cottage, Gerda hurried to the kitchen to make a pot of tea. Olina was glad that she and Gerda had baked Christmas cookies the day before.

Mrs. Sandstrom and Olina sat on the sofa holding hands and devouring each other with their eyes. "Mother, what are you doing here?"

Brigitta laughed at her daughter. "I've come to help plan a wedding." She pulled Olina into another hug. "Have you set a date yet?"

Olina leaned back from her mother's arms. "I wanted to wait until I heard from Fader. Where is he?"

After standing up, Mrs. Sandstrom paced once across the parlor. With her back still turned toward her daughter, she started explaining. "Your father couldn't come, Olina." She turned around and looked into Olina's face. "I brought some bad news."

Oh no. Please God. Her thoughts became jumbled. She wasn't even sure what she was asking Him for. She had realized when Moder didn't tell her anything in town that something bad had happened, but she hadn't wanted to believe it was possible. Now she could no longer deny it.

Mrs. Sandstrom crossed the room and sat beside her daughter. "There's no easy way to say this. Your father became sick. I believe it was his hard-heartedness toward you that brought the sickness on. I prayed for him so much, but he kept getting sicker and sicker."

She pulled a hanky from her sleeve and wiped the tears that were making trails down her cheeks. That caused Olina to realize how wrinkled they had become. As she looked closer at her mother, Olina realized that she had lost weight, and her hair, which had still retained the golden color when Olina last saw her a month before she left Sweden, was streaked with silver. When had her mother become old? It had only been nine months since Olina last saw her. Nine months shouldn't have done that much damage. Unless something terrible had happened.

"Finally, your father told me that we must contact you. He wanted to make peace with you. I told him that I would write you a letter the next morning, but before the sun came up, he left us."

Olina pulled her mother into her arms, and the two women cried together. They weren't aware of Gerda entering the room, but when they stopped crying, they found a tray—with a pot of tea, two cups and saucers, and some cookies—sitting on the table in front of the sofa. Olina poured each of them a cup of tea, but neither of them picked up a cookie.

After taking a few sips from the bracing brew, Mrs. Sandstrom set her cup and saucer back on the table. "That day, we received your letter telling about Gustaf and asking your father to forgive you. I'm so sorry he wasn't able to say this himself, but I know that he would accept your apology and welcome you back into the family."

Olina smiled at her mother through her tears. "I hope so. I wouldn't set a date for the wedding, because I was waiting to hear from Fader."

Mrs. Sandstrom patted Olina on the knee. "I know, Dear. That is why Tant Olga urged me to come to America and talk to you in person."

Olina smiled. "Tant Olga?"

"Ja, for sure." Mrs. Sandstrom returned her smile. "I already turned the farm over to the boys. When Sven got so sick, I couldn't help them at all. All my time was taken with caring for him. Then he died, and Olga asked me to live with her. That way the boys would know that the farm is theirs. Sven and I saved enough money for me to live on for the rest of my life. I won't have many expenses living with Olga, and she needs me."

Olina looked up as Gerda came into the parlor with a carpetbag in her hand. "Are you going somewhere?"

Gerda went over and hugged Mrs. Sandstrom, then Olina. "I wanted to give you and your mother some time alone. August put her luggage in my room. He and I have been having tea in the kitchen. Now he'll take me home. I'll stay with my parents for a few days."

Mrs. Sandstrom stood up. "You don't have to do that, Gerda. I can sleep here on the sofa."

"No need for that." Gerda turned and called August. "I'm ready to go."

August came in and took the carpetbag from her. Then he helped her into her heavy coat. "It's cold. You probably should take a blanket to wrap up in during the drive."

Gerda went upstairs and returned quickly with the cover. "Don't be surprised if Gustaf comes for dinner tonight. I'm sure he'll want to be with the two of you."

After Gerda and August left, Olina and her mother planned

a special meal for when Gustaf came. It was good to work together in the kitchen again. Gustaf arrived as they were putting the finishing touches on the food.

Olina answered his knock. He gave her a quick hug before he greeted her mother. Soon they were seated at the table sharing the special meal.

"How long are you staying in Minnesota?" Gustaf asked.

"I planned to stay for awhile. It's such a long journey. One of my cousins is staying with Tant Olga until I return." Brigitta glanced at her daughter. "I want to be here for the wedding, and I know Olina needs some time to mourn her father's death."

Gustaf put his fork down and looked from mother to daughter. "For sure, that's right. I know Olina was anxious to hear from him." He reached over and placed his hand on Olina's shoulder. "How are you doing?"

Olina's eyes glistened with unshed tears. "I'll be okay. It will just take some time."

"I want to be here for the wedding." Brigitta took a bite of the gräddbakelse she had made because it was such a favorite of Olina's.

"Maybe we should set the date tonight." Gustaf studied Olina for a moment. "Do you think we could do that?"

"Moder, can you stay until April?" Olina asked.

"Ja, for sure."

Gustaf and Olina soon decided that they would exchange their vows on Saturday, April 9. That would give them plenty of time to plan the wedding, and Olina and her mother would have time to enjoy each other.

❧

Since Christmas was only a few days away, Gerda and Olina were busy with a few last-minute orders for Christmas presents. Gustaf brought Gerda to the house every morning, so she and Olina could work together. After two days, he took

Mrs. Sandstrom back to the farm with him to visit with her old friend, Ingrid.

That day Gerda and Olina went to town to purchase fabric so they could make Mrs. Sandstrom a suit similar to the one they were making Mrs. Nilsson. They finished in time for the family Christmas at the farm.

❧

Olina woke on her wedding day to the sun streaming through her window. She was used to getting up at dawn and making breakfast, but Gerda must have beaten her to it. The fragrant aroma of coffee beckoned Olina to the warm kitchen.

"Well, Sleepyhead, I see you finally woke up." Gerda was pouring a cup of coffee as Olina entered the room.

"Yes. I didn't think I would ever go to sleep. I was so excited thinking about today." Olina stretched and yawned before she sat at the place Gerda set for her at the table. "When I did go to sleep, I slept like a baby." Gerda placed a plate filled with pancakes and sausage in front of Olina.

Olina gasped. It was so much food. "I can't eat all of this."

"You need to," Gerda urged. "You might not be able to eat lunch, and you must keep up your strength. I don't want you fainting before you walk down the aisle."

It was here. Her wedding day. Olina could hardly believe it. So much had gone into the preparations for the day. Her mother wanted to make her wedding dress. Olina and Gerda told Mrs. Sandstrom that she should learn to use the sewing machine, but she insisted on making the dress by hand. Her stitches were tiny and even, a labor of love.

The wedding was scheduled for one o'clock, because Gustaf and Olina were catching the four o'clock train. They were taking a honeymoon trip to San Francisco.

❧

Gustaf stood beside the preacher at the front of the church.

His father was standing at the back of the church with Olina's dainty hand resting on his arm. Since her father wasn't there to escort her down the aisle, she asked Gustaf's father. It made both Bennel and Gustaf very proud.

Gustaf caught his breath at the vision of loveliness. Olina wore a dress of white silk brocade. A single row of flowers, formed into a coronet, now adorned her golden tresses. She looked like an angel. His angel.

Tears formed in his eyes. *Thank You, Father, for bringing her to me.*

The pastor's wife began playing the organ, and Olina walked toward him.

I'll care for her, Father, as You have cared for me. I'll love her and cherish her.

Olina had never seen the suit Gustaf was wearing. He must have bought a new one for the wedding. She was amused. He wore a suit so seldom, but it meant a lot to her that he would purchase a new suit for their wedding. He was such a thoughtful man.

As Olina and Mr. Nilsson walked down the aisle, tears blurred Olina's vision. It didn't matter that she couldn't really see the people who surrounded them. *Father, thank You for what You planned for me. Thank You for helping me come to the place that I could recognize Your plans. I will love and cherish Gustaf for the rest of my life.*

A Letter To Our Readers

Dear Reader:

In order that we might better contribute to your reading enjoyment, we would appreciate your taking a few minutes to respond to the following questions. We welcome your comments and read each form and letter we receive. When completed, please return to the following:

Rebecca Germany, Fiction Editor
Heartsong Presents
PO Box 719
Uhrichsville, Ohio 44683

1. Did you enjoy reading *The Other Brother* by Lena Nelson Dooley?
   - ❏ Very much! I would like to see more books by this author!
   - ❏ Moderately. I would have enjoyed it more if

   _____

   _____

2. Are you a member of **Heartsong Presents**? Yes ❏ No ❏
   If no, where did you purchase this book?_____

   _____

3. How would you rate, on a scale from 1 (poor) to 5 (superior), the cover design?_____

4. On a scale from 1 (poor) to 10 (superior), please rate the following elements.

   _____ Heroine   _____ Plot

   _____ Hero   _____ Inspirational theme

   _____ Setting   _____ Secondary characters

5. These characters were special because _____

_____

_____

6. How has this book inspired your life? _____

_____

_____

7. What settings would you like to see covered in future **Heartsong Presents** books? _____

_____

_____

8. What are some inspirational themes you would like to see treated in future books? _____

_____

_____

9. Would you be interested in reading other **Heartsong Presents** titles? Yes ❑ No ❑

10. Please check your age range:
    ❑ Under 18 ❑ 18-24 ❑ 25-34
    ❑ 35-45 ❑ 46-55 ❑ Over 55

Name _____

Occupation _____

Address _____

City _____ State _____ Zip _____

Email _____

Pennsylvania

The pristine woods of Pennsylvania beckon, and adventurous souls make a perilous journey to the New World.

Follow two pioneer families as they tame the American wilderness and pursue the desires of their hearts. What godly legacy will each person leave?

paperback, 480 pages, 5 $\frac{3}{16}$" x 8"

·····Hearts♥ng·····

HISTORICAL ROMANCE IS CHEAPER BY THE DOZEN!

Any 12 *Heartsong Presents* titles for only $27.00 *

Buy any assortment of twelve *Heartsong Presents* titles and save 25% off of the already discounted price of $2.95 each!

*plus $2.00 shipping and handling per order and sales tax where applicable.

HEARTSONG PRESENTS TITLES AVAILABLE NOW: